NICK NELSON WAS HERE

A NOVEL

Matt Micros

For everyone who believes in true love

Also by Matt Micros

~Five Days~

~The Knights of Redemption~

~The Chameleon~

TABLE OF CONTENTS

I	*The Last of the Nice Guys*	*11*
II	*Mr. McDermott*	*21*
III	*It's Called a Tombstone*	*31*
IV	*Heaven and Hell*	*38*
V	*The Closer and the Big Fish*	*47*
VI	*The Truth Teller*	*53*
VII	*Shameless*	*66*
VIII	*A Trooper, a Pan and a Road Trip*	*75*
IX	*The World According to Rick*	*83*
X	*Middle America*	*88*
XI	*The Search Begins*	*93*
XII	*Riverboat Gamblers*	*105*
XIII	*The Voice of an Angel*	*112*
XIV	*Reunited at Long Last*	*122*
XV	*A Dish Best Served Cold*	*131*
XVI	*Climbing Multnomah*	*141*
XVII	*Better Than He Thought He Was*	*149*
XVIII	*Nice Guys Don't Always Finish Last*	*153*

NICK NELSON WAS HERE

"There is only one kind of love, but there are a thousand imitations."

La Rochefoucauld

I   THE LAST OF THE NICE GUYS

Nick Nelson was first brandished with the moniker "the last of the nice guys" after leaving a pickup basketball game in 6th grade to help an elderly lady he didn't know, carry her groceries 17 blocks to her house. He did little to change that view of him when he went to his Senior Prom with a girl in a wheelchair, and he cemented it forevermore after driving his roommate's one night stand home *for* him, when his roommate got called into work. He even bought her breakfast on the way.

The label was something he was neither proud of, nor abhorred, for he knew the title and a quarter would only get him a phone call at a pay phone. But it was also his even keeled personality that enabled him to brush off days that would have driven a lessor person wild.

~

The line at the tax office was ten deep as it usually was at the end of the month. An array of people of varying ages and economic stature waited; some patiently, others, not so much.

"I'm here to pay my son's car tax," an elderly woman announced to no one in particular. She was a kindly looking woman, well-dressed, with curly white hair and soft skin.

"Is he in high school?" another woman asked, the slight tilt of her head indicating that she wondered how a woman in her seventies could have a teenage son.

"Oh, no," the elderly woman responded. "He's 41, but he lives at home with us. So does his brother who's 47."

"Neither of them is married?"

"They've never been. They have it pretty good. We don't make them pay rent, and I cook for them. They have plenty of money to spend as they choose."

An older man entered the conversation at that point. His tightly cropped hair and posture that was much straighter than normal for someone his age, led Nick to believe he might be a veteran.

"Smart boys. A little ice cream ain't worth 40 years of misery," he said.

Nick, silent until that point, spit the water he was sipping across the floor. Nick Nelson was average in nearly every manner used to describe a person physically except for one. He had abnormally large feet. He credited that feature for the first of his two self-proclaimed talents—his ability to fall asleep anywhere, at any time--even while standing up; and his ability to listen in on other people's conversations without making it seem as though he was. Although spitting the water onto the linoleum tiles of the tax office left some question about his second talent.

"I don't think I'd ever get married again," the second woman said, as if she was hoping Nick would try to talk her out of it.

"No?" Nick asked politely. The woman had probably been pretty at one time, but life seemed to have worn her down. She wasn't particularly heavy, yet not tone either, and her tan skin had a sort of leatherette look to it, as if it needed to be sanded down first before color was applied. She was probably in her late-thirties, but appeared much older. The fact that she was there in the middle of the day and the fact that her tan was much darker than a two-day weekend tan, told him that she worked nights, most likely at a grocery store or something of that nature.

"What about you? Have you ever been married?" she asked.

"Not yet. Still fighting the good fight."

The crusty vet winked and nodded his approval, while his wife, having recently joined him in line, slapped him across the arm, causing him to roll his eyes.

"I'm not opposed to it," Nick added almost as an afterthought. "But she would have to be a pretty special woman."

"Don't say a word!" the vet's wife responded before her husband could.

The conversation was interrupted by the screaming of a two year old boy, whose three year old brother had just pushed him over. When his young mother reprimanded him, the three year old began to pound his forehead off the floor.

"Matthew! No!" she shouted desperately as she tried to pull him from the floor.

"My parents told me I used to bang my head on the floor when I was little," Nick offered.

"I'm worried he's going to hurt himself," she answered as he wriggled free from her grasp.

"Well, I wouldn't encourage it," Nick said with a smile, "but I turned out ok."

"Next," the woman at window 2 said, her eyes widening to indicate she was ready for Nick.

"How are you?" he said as he approached.

"How can I help you?" she answered in a tone that expressed she had little desire to do exactly that.

"I'm just looking to pick up a couple of beach parking stickers."

"Do you have your license and registration with you?"

"My license, yes. I didn't think I needed my registration."

"I should be able to pull it up on the computer. What's the plate number?"

"I have two cars actually, and ummm....neither have personalized plates, so I don't really know the plate numbers to be honest."

"What's your address?" the woman droned.

"Same as on my driver's license," Nick answered with a smile.

She punched in a few keys, then stared blankly at the screen for a moment or two. "I don't have any cars registered to you in Stamford," she said at last.

"I have two of them. One's parked out front," Nick reassured her.

"I see a blue Hummer registered to you in Fairfield."

"That's where I used to live."

"Did you ever transfer over the registration?"

His lack of a response told her the answer was no.

"I didn't know I had to," he answered at last. "But the other car should definitely be in there. I bought it long after I moved. I've only had it for two months."

"Well, that's why it's not showing up in the system then. They update it every six months. You said you have that car with you?"

"Yes. It's out front."

"Can you go get the registration?"

Nick looked at her and then at the ever-growing line that had now spilled out into the corridor.

"I'll give you a pass to come right to the window," she said in the tone of an irritated high school teacher.

"Thank you," he said as he took the pass. "I'll be right back."

When he returned, the young woman with the two young boys was still a good five people away from the window. She seemed to be at her last wit. Nick took a deep breath and handed her his pass as if it was the golden ticket to get into the Chocolate Factory. She took it gratefully. The woman at the window scowled at Nick. The passes were supposed to be non-transferable, but she was tired of listening to the boy pound his head off the floor as well, so she let it slide.

Thirty minutes later, Nick was finally at the window again. He handed her his registration, which she studied carefully.

"This is a temporary registration," she said.

"It's what they gave me," Nick explained.

"It's expired."

"I haven't received a permanent one yet."

"I can't accept this."

"Are you serious?"

"Yes, I'm serious. You have one car whose registration has expired and another not even registered in town."

"My driver's license is up to date and I promise you both cars made the trip to Stamford with me. I didn't leave them behind."

"You live on Beach Avenue. Why do you even need beach stickers anyway?' the woman asked.

"Well, that's actually kind of a long story," Nick began. "You see, a few weeks ago, I had my roof redone, and the guys doing it used a big tree I had in the yard as a scaffold to work on certain areas of the roof. Anyway, about a week later, in the middle of the night, I heard this huge crash, and looked out the window to see that the tree had fallen into the street. Well, the Public Works guys didn't chop the tree up for me. They simply picked it up and tossed it back into my yard. So, I then had to hire someone to come out, chop the tree up and grind up the stump. While they were doing that, their huge wood-chipper truck, chipped my driveway. That chip soon became a sinkhole. So, I had to get an engineer out and he said I needed to get it repaired as soon as possible and he recommended having the entire driveway redone. They're doing that as we speak, but I won't be able to drive on it for a couple of days, so I have to park my cars in the lot down the street. I wanted the beach stickers so I could park there without getting a bunch of parking tickets."

Most people, after hearing a story like that, would have relented and handed over the stickers. "Sorry I'm afraid I can't help you," the woman answered before turning to the next person in line. "Next."

At that point, some people would have responded with a string of expletives and thrown something. Nick merely nodded his head as if her response made sense and walked silently from the office.

He took a deep breath once outside. He loved the smells and sounds of late summer. Freshly cut grass. Flowers on their second bloom. The tide rolling in. He opened the passenger door of his car and placed his expired, temporary registration certificate inside the glove compartment before walking around to the other side. On the windshield was a canary yellow parking ticket. He had exceeded the 60 minute allotment. Many people at this point would have torn the ticket to bits and left the pieces on the street. Nick tossed it onto his passenger seat.

"Nice car," a voice said from behind him.

He looked up and saw the woman with the leatherette skin from the tax office waiting at the bus stop. "Thanks," he answered. "I just got it a couple of months ago."

"A Porsche, right?"

"Yes," he answered, almost embarrassedly.

"You can definitely tell you're not married," the woman laughed.

"Yeah, I figured I'd have my mid-life crisis a little early. You need a ride?" Nick asked.

"I don't want to put you out."

"You're not putting me out.   I've got nowhere in particular to be."

"Well, I never have ridden in a Porsche," the woman said as she climbed in. "I'm Cheryl."

"Nick," he answered, formally introducing himself for the first time. "Where to, Cheryl?"

"The Super Stop & Shop over by the mall. I really appreciate this.   I'm supposed to be at work by 4:30, and I think I'd be late if I had to wait for the next bus."

"No problem."

"So what do you do for a living?" she asked.

"I'm a producer for a small town Saturday morning television talk show called *Fairfield County Weekly*."

"I've heard of it, but never seen it," she said politely.   He figured she had probably never even heard of it.

"Yeah, it's got kind of a small audience."

"It can't be that small if you're driving a car like this," she remarked.

"Like I said, I'm single. No wife. No kids," he laughed.

"There's Margie!" the woman exclaimed as they pulled into the parking lot. "Do you think you could do me a favor and drop me off in the front?   She'll shit gold bricks if she sees me getting out of this car."

"Well, let's hope she does," Nick said.   "Gold bricks are very valuable."

"You know, the Oyster Fest is this weekend," Cheryl said as she scribbled a number on the back of a business card. "If you're around, give me a call."

"Thanks. If I'm around, I will."

"Thanks again for the ride."

"You're welcome."

He flipped over the card. It was a salesman's card for office supplies. The guy must have given it to her. Now she had given it to him. It was wonder anyone ever got married. She was nice enough, but not his type. If he ever walked down the aisle, he wanted it to be with someone that was also experiencing it for the first time as well. He would toss the card in the "if I'm lonely and desperate box" in his kitchen when he got home.

The pavers were just finishing up at his house as he pulled up to the curb. He had to admit. The driveway did look nice.

"All finished?" Nick asked.

"Yeah. You can walk on it, but I wouldn't drive on it for a couple of days. And I would make sure any fat friends go in through the front door," the gruff paver responded.

"Here's your money," Nick said, handing him an envelope of cash.

"Thanks. We filled that hole pretty good and paved up a solid two inches. You should be all set now."

"Great."

Nick looked at his house as the trucks pulled away. It had been his dream house for years, and when it finally went on sale three years ago, he jumped at the opportunity.

The house was a large white colonial, much larger than needed for a single person, with gleaming round pillars anchoring it in the front and sliding glass doors on both levels opening to a spectacular view of the Long Island Sound out back. The yard was meticulously kept, with a four-foot boxwood hedge shielding it from outsiders. He did notice, however, that the grass was getting a bit unruly. Nick went over to the crawlspace where he stored his lawnmower and pulled on the door. It wouldn't open. He pulled again, harder this time and it opened slightly before jamming. Nick looked down and shook his head in amazement. The pavers had paved in his crawlspace.

At this point, most people would have embarked on a five state killing spree. But Nick Nelson was not most people. Instead, the last of the nice guys merely chuckled, his chuckle soon becoming a hearty laugh at the absurdity of it all.

II MR. MCDERMOTT

*T*he words "nice guy" and "Rick McDermott" rarely found their way into the same sentence and it didn't seem to bother Rick at all. With his sardonic wit, searing sarcasm and occasional charm, he was nearly always the highlight of any gathering—unless of course, you were the focus of his venom.

An All-American First Baseman at the University of Notre Dame, he had earned his M.B.A. at Yale after graduation, and soon found himself an employee of Pressman-Griggs—the most successful advertising firm in New York City. If you ate it, wore it or wiped with it, chances are they represented it. After 15 years, Rick was a Senior Advertising Executive, the man they always sent in to close the deal or come up with a campaign slogan when everyone else was blocked. He was arguably the most valuable member of the firm, and yet had been passed over for partner on several occasions for the simple reason that Bill Griggs hated him.

On a good day, Rick referred to Griggs as "that goofy bastard". On a bad one, Griggs was a "pansy-ass, no talent, useless, waste of space, goofy bastard". The two of them had hated each other almost from the moment they met. He saw Griggs for what he was—someone who had ridden on the coat tails of his older and more famous partner. Instead of being grateful for having been brought along for the ride, he was jealous and resentful. Rick saw him for what he was and it irritated Griggs to no end.

On several occasions, Griggs had tried to fire him, but Rick simply brought in too much money for Pressman to even consider it. Why Rick stayed where he wasn't wanted was the simple mathematical equation of self-employment equals less money plus more aggravation. Translation: It was easier to stay where he was. In a few more years, he would have enough money to retire with homes in Sullivan Island, Nantucket, and the Gold Coast of Connecticut, in addition to apartments in New York City and Southern Italy. He didn't love his job, although there was a time when he did. Rick found that the higher profile the client, the less they were willing to listen. His job had become less about creating and more about telling them what they wanted to hear. He had developed the innate ability to immediately sense what people wanted to hear and regurgitate it back to them as if the idea had been their own.

"Brilliant!" they would respond as Rick simply shook his head and collected his paycheck.

He walked into the offices of Pressman-Griggs at 9:15am, or exactly fifteen minutes later than he was supposed to arrive. On most days he was in the building well before nine, but he knew his coming in late, irritated Griggs, so he would either stay downstairs and converse with the security guard or get a leisurely coffee in the café.

"Morning, Joan," he said to his secretary as he entered his office.

"Good morning, Mr. McDermott," she answered. "Don't forget you have a meeting with Mr. Griggs at 9:30."

"How could I forget?" Rick mumbled as he tossed his briefcase on the couch and headed back down the corridor.

He waited in Griggs' office for the better part of twenty minutes. He pulled out his IPhone and checked the stock market. The weather. His email. Read every article on the New York Mets website. Sent a couple of obnoxious text messages to co-workers. When he had exhausted every gadget on the phone, he gave up waiting and left.

He stuck his head in the office a few doors down. "You ready to go to lunch?" he asked a man who was working on a storyboard. The man was in his thirties, not as good looking as Rick, but with an appearance that was much neater. His shirt and pants were neatly pressed. His tie was precisely to the bottom of his belt buckle. His shoes were spit-shined to a nice glossy finish.

"It's 10:00 in the morning," the man answered without looking up.

"So? They don't appreciate us enough around here."

"They don't appreciate us around here *because* you go to lunch at 10:00 and they know we're friends. Guilt by association."

"So you're saying it's my fault you're not a partner yet? Man, my back is killin me from carrying you on it for the past fifteen years!" Rick said.

Tom laughed. "I'm saying *you're* not a partner because you arrive late, take early lunches, don't wear a tie most days, leave early, and have no respect whatsoever for authority."

"I have respect for my mother—the only woman I truly trust," Rick announced. "Now, about lunch...."

There was some truth to what Rick had said. The two had met in business school, and were it not for Rick, Tom Reynolds might never have passed his graduate thesis. Then when it came time to interview for jobs, Rick made it a two for one at Pressman-Griggs. He said he wouldn't come without Tom. The partners reluctantly agreed and a day rarely passed where at least Bill Griggs didn't regret it. He liked Tom well enough. Tom was enough of a "yes" man to suit him, but Rick was another story.

"So I waited for him in his office for like twenty minutes and the fucking guy never showed up. Goofy lookin, no talent, waste of space that he is," Rick explained while he and Tom ate a couple of Italian sausages in Central Park. "Good, no? Kind of like a breakfast sandwich."

The wrinkles in Tom's forehead said it all. "Not exactly. So what did he want to meet about this time?"

"Same shit. The guy literally clocks me in in the morning and out at night. It's to the point now where if I'm early, I'll wait downstairs until I'm late. And then he goes on and on about wearing a tie. I don't want to wear a tie. I can't think when I have something tight around my neck. And our clients don't give a shit if I'm wearing a tie or not. They want to know if I can sell their product. They wouldn't care if I made the presentation naked as long as sales went up. Hell, some of the guys that work for Cosmel Cosmetics would probably like it."

"Wow, that's completely offensive, and yet, not altogether surprising coming from you."

"Did you just join GLAAD or something?"

"You don't have to be gay to be offended at some of the things you say," Tom explained.

"Well, I'm sure it would help," Rick shrugged.

His secretary informed him once he had returned to the office that Bill Griggs wanted to see him immediately. Rick knew as soon as he walked into Bill's office and saw John Pressman seated in there, that there was something different about this meeting.

"John. Bill," Rick nodded.

"We need to talk, Rick," Pressman began as Bill sat with a growingly smug look on his face.

"About?"

"A number of things really. Tardiness. Your appearance. A lack of respect for one of the partners. Some of this is my fault. I've let it go for too long because you brought in a lot of business."

"John, you're a businessman. And because of that, I think this is a fair question. Which would you rather have? Someone who arrives a few minutes late, and leaves a few minutes early on occasion, but brings in thousands and thousands of dollars worth of business? Or someone who's there all the time, but can't get out of their own way?"

"Why can't I have both?"

It was a fair response, and one that Rick didn't quite know how to answer. After all, it was his company. He had the right to demand whatever he wanted.

"The bigger issue, is that on one hand, I have a partner that I started the company with, who has helped me build this agency into one of the top agencies in the world—"

"He hasn't helped that much," Rick interjected.

"And on the other," Pressman continued, "I have my top executive, a guy who's brought in a lot of business, *a lot.* And, the two of them can't stand each other. Now you tell me what I'm supposed to do."

"I know what I would do," Rick answered. "I'd buy the goofy bastard out before your top executive leaves with half your client roster and your company goes bankrupt."

"Do you think this is a joke?" Pressman said as he uncharacteristically raised his voiced.

"No, I think it's tragic."

"You don't even have enough respect for one of the partners to show up for a meeting with him?"

"I showed up at 9:30 and waited for about twenty minutes before leaving."

"The meeting was at 11:00," Griggs said. They were the first words he had spoken.

"No, it was at 9:30. You changed it to that time I assume, because you wanted to make sure I was in the building early in the morning."

"The meeting was at 11:00, and you weren't even in the building. You were out getting lunch."

Rick grabbed the phone that was in the center of the conference table, dialed an extension, and put the call on speakerphone. It was his voicemail. He punched in a code and a message began to play.

"This is Jana in Bill Griggs office. Bill wanted me to remind you that your meeting with him is at 9:30am tomorrow. Thanks."

"That was before we changed the time," Griggs said indignantly.

Rick nodded as he reached into his shirt pocket and removed a phone message that read, *"Meeting changed to 9:30. Bill."*

"Not only are you a goofy looking, no talent, waste of space, but you're a fucking liar," Rick answered as he threw the message in Griggs's face.

Griggs looked like he wanted to go up over the table at him.

"Gentlemen, and I use that term loosely, enough!" Pressman said angrily. "Bill, leave us for a minute."

"What?!" Griggs said, astonished.

"Nothing is going to get accomplished with both of you here, so let me talk to you both separately."

Griggs reluctantly trudged from his own office. Rick winked at him and waved on his way out.

"Rick. I sit here with you and I could see us having a drink and talking about world events. But for some reason, you and Bill are like oil and water."

"Look, we both know the real reason he's had it out for me is because Johnson & Johnson wanted me to take over their campaign from his son. And we both also know I did everything I could to keep him involved."

"That may be, but the question remains. How are we going to work this out to best benefit the company? You should already be a partner by now. But I can't go over his head and make you one without you at least trying to meet him halfway. I've spent the last fifteen years fighting with him just to keep you, because you're talented."

"I appreciate that," Rick said. "And you're right. I should be a partner by now. As for what we're going to do to make this work, that's easy. I quit."

"Let's not make a hasty decision," Pressman said, backtracking a bit.

"John, you're a good man, and I appreciate the opportunity you've given me, but you could offer to pave the streets with gold and line them with beautiful women throwing rose petals at me while I ride in on a chariot that you sent to bring me to work, and I still wouldn't come back here tomorrow."

Rick left the elder statesman of the firm with his mouth agape as he walked out the door. "Hey, Bill," he said as he walked past, "go fuck yourself."

Fifteen years there and it took him all of five minutes to pack up his things. He didn't have a wife or kids. No nieces or nephews. Just a picture of his parents, five or six pictures of Tom and him at the Mets Fantasy Camp in which Rick was named Camp MVP, and a couple of Emmy-like advertising awards that he had stuffed into the bottom drawer of his desk.

"You coming?" Rick asked as he stood in

Tom's doorway holding his box of belongings.

"Coming where?" Tom asked, without looking up.

"I quit."

"You what?!" Tom asked in a fury, looking up this time.

"He quit!" came the response from the younger man standing over Rick's right shoulder. Another younger associate stood to his left. "Told Bill Griggs to go fuck himself."

"I was ten feet away. It was beautiful." The second man added.

"We're leaving to form our own firm, *The Adgency*," Rick said. "We'll have four partners. McDermott, Jones, Vossler....and Reynolds if you're in."

Tom glanced at the picture on his desk of his wife and children. Then he looked at the five or so pictures he had of him and Rick sitting on an end table. It took him about fifteen seconds before he dumped out a file box and began tossing his personal items in it—which was about fifteen seconds before security arrived to escort them all from the premises.

As they stepped through the security held-open door of the building, the warm summer air enveloped them, along with a sudden sense of panic at what they were going to do next.

"How are we going to reach any of the clients?" Tom asked. "They wouldn't let us take any of our contact information."

"Relax," Rick answered calmly. "I've been emailing that info to my home computer for the past month."

"You *knew* you were going to do this?!"

"I didn't *know*. But I am kind of a prick, so I

always considered it a possibility," he said as the four of them continued down the busy Manhattan sidewalk.

III   IT'S CALLED A TOMBSTONE

Rick didn't need to move his glove one inch as the softball that had been fired from the 3rd baseman landed in it with a smack.

"Who's Nettles?" he asked Tom as he tossed the ball to the catcher.

"One of Jerry's friends. Nick something or other. He's a television producer."

"He ever play any ball?"

"High school I think. He wasn't a big college star like you," Tom said with a smirk.

"Not many people were, my friend. Not many people were."

There was a fundamental difference between men and women that was illustrated that morning. Whereas women took a while to warm up to someone new, it only took Nick making a diving stop to preserve a one run lead in the last inning for he and Rick to become chest-bumping best friends forever.

"You never played any college ball?" Rick asked as they took their stuff off after the game. "I'm Rick McDermott by the way."

"Nick Nelson," Nick answered, shaking his hand. "High school only. I hated batting. I was always afraid of getting hit. The first time I ever faced a curve ball, I threw my bat in the air and dove backwards out of the way, just as the ball broke across the plate for a strike. The place erupted in laughter as I picked the dirt out of my teeth."

"You big pussy," Rick smiled. "With your glove, you'd be in the major leagues today."

"Maybe if they had a designated *fielder*," Nick laughed. "I think slo-pitch softball is more my speed."

"Tom and I are going to get a couple of beers. You want to join us?"

"Sure. I live right around the corner. I just have to walk home and get my car."

"Jump in with us," Tom offered. "We'll bring you back."

Having a beer on an outdoor patio bar with Rick and Tom while the Mets game played in the background, took Nick back to a time when he actually had friends. All the way through his mid-twenties, Nick had people he could hang out with. But eventually, they all got married, and before he knew it, he found that he was the last remaining bachelor on earth. Or so it seemed. Nowadays he had acquaintances. People he knew from work and former friends who would call him up when their wives were away. But no one he would feel comfortable calling if his car broke down in the middle of the night.

"So you're a TV producer, huh?" Rick asked.

"Yeah."

"For what show?"

"A local gabfest called *Fairfield County Weekly*. We have writers, singers and politicians for guests and talk about anything exciting going on in the area."

"I've never seen it, but then again I live in

the city."

"Any big names come on?" Tom asked.

"John Mayer came on once because he's from the area. So did James Blake the tennis player. But mostly just people like the First Selectman from District Four in Wilton," Nick laughed. "How bout you guys? What do you do?"

"Well until Friday, we both worked for Pressman-Griggs," Rick answered between chugs.

"The advertising agency?"

They both nodded.

"But then Rick told Griggs to go fuck himself and three of us stupidly decided to follow him out the door."

"I prefer to think of us now as gainfully *un*employed. Addition by subtraction," Rick said.

"Yes, subtraction of our income."

"We'll be fine. Just leave it to me."

It was amazing how different people could have such differing views of the same person. To most people, Rick McDermott was brash and arrogant. Nick found him humorous and confident. Others saw him as rude. Nick considered him benevolently challenged. Some found him explosive and unpredictable. Nick thought he was passionate and spontaneous. It was safe to say he liked him very much.

Rick never delved that deeply into people's personalities. They simply fell into one of two categories. Good guys and assholes. Women were in a category all their own and he seemed to be texting one of them while they drank.

"You text more than a high school girl," Nick

laughed.

"That's because he's dating one," Tom chimed in.

"She's not in high school," Rick corrected without an ounce of embarrassment.

"Sorry. College."

"You're dating a college girl? What are you? 36?"

"37."

"You're the man."

"Yes, he's the man," Tom said sarcastically. "Ask him about his theory on women and dating."

"I'll bite. What's your theory on women and dating?"

"It's very simple really," Rick began. "Women are only good for one thing. Two, if they can cook. But men make better friends. So if I'm going to go to a ball game or something, I'd rather take a guy. If I'm looking for a little sumthin sumthin, then I'll call a woman. The problem is, women our age are either married, divorced, or carrying some serious baggage. So you have to look for younger women."

"20 year olds," Nick offered.

"Exactly. They're fun. They're not looking to get married. And the sex is great."

"But how many 20 year olds are going to want to date guys like us?"

"Tons of them. They love guys who can take them out to the bars, to a Broadway play, maybe a vacation to Cabo. Things that guys their age can't do yet."

"Ok, so you find this girl. Then what?"

"Then you date for a while. Eventually, they'll realize they'd end up spending the last five years of *your* life feeding you through a straw and the last fifteen of *theirs* alone with two kids, so they settle down with someone their own age."

"And what do you do then?"

"You find another 20 year old. If need be, you can settle for a 25 year old. But you have to make sure they aren't looking to get married. So no Mormons."

"Of course not," Nick nodded as if that made sense. He was greatly amused. "But what happens when you get older? You can't date 25 year olds forever."

"You can try. I'll let you in on a secret. The oldest woman I've ever slept with is 26."

"You have got to be kidding me."

"He's not," Tom assured him.

"The last three women I've dated have been 20, 24 and 23. When I was 30, I dated the 26 year old. That didn't last long. But if necessary, you can always move up an age group and date a 30 year old. Now that's like shooting fish in a barrel. Either they're single and desperate. Or they're divorced with kids and even more desperate."

"And you marry one of them?"

"Of course not. I don't ever want to get married. Once the sex drive is gone, I'll follow the Mets around Florida for spring training and travel to Europe."

"Wow. Not me. I'd like to have a family some day," Nick said. "The thing is, my whole life, I've always thought that I was going to find this storybook romance. Something amazing. Something special that no one else had. And so I kept holding out and I let some great girls go.

It wasn't like I thought I was any great shakes or anything. I just kept waiting for the lightning bolt, and it never came. Year after year, I watched each of my buddies get married, and before you knew it, it was just me. Now, I think that maybe there is no such thing as falling in love. That maybe the best I can do is find someone I like."

"Exactly my point," Rick reiterated. "Have a little sex, hang out with your guy friends, and enjoy life."

"Don't listen to him," Tom said. "He's the same guy who turned down an invitation to his senior prom by the beautiful Grey Poupon mustard heiress so he could go get drunk in the parking lot with his buddies."

"I don't know what to think anymore. I mean, and I know this is going to sound soft, but when I was younger, there was no greater feeling than the feeling you had when you first realized that the girl you liked felt the same way about you. That moment," Nick said, gesturing with his hands for emphasis, "that feeling—was the greatest feeling in the world."

"It's called the Principle of the Moment," Tom said. "I read that somewhere."

Rick rolled his eyes, "It's called the Principle of Stupidity."

A couple of hours later, they dropped Nick off at the sprawling, white home on the beach.

"Did you say you're a producer for the *Today Show*?" Tom asked, stunned at how beautiful the house was.

"Now *this*, is a house twenty year olds would like," Rick added.

"I don't think he's looking to turn it into a

frat house."

"Who said anything about a frat? I was thinking more along the lines of a sorority."

"How do you afford this, if you don't mind my asking?" Tom asked.

"The downside of being single is that I'll probably die alone. The upside is that I don't have a wife or kids to support. It's only me," Nick answered.

"I'm single and I don't have a place like this!" Rick exclaimed.

"Don't listen to him. He's got four of them," Tom interjected.

"I figured it would be a good place to raise a family someday."

"Oh god, not that again," Rick grimaced.

"What can I say? I'd like to have kids," Nick said. "When I leave this earth, I want to leave something behind that says, *Nick Nelson was here.*"

"You will," Rick assured him. "It's called a tombstone."

IV   HEAVEN AND HELL

No matter how organized and prepared you were, the fifteen minutes before a live television show began was always complete and utter chaos.

"Where's Ben Weiner?" Nick shouted to the entire studio.

"He's stuck in traf-fic," was the sing-songy, yet calm response from his student intern. Katy was nearing her graduation at Poquonac University, a school best known for its political polls, but one that had a growing communications school as well. She had worked for Nick all spring as an intern, but was set to graduate in a week. Katy was tall, thin and pretty with very little effort. She wore glasses and had a large mop of blondish brown hair in a loose bun that was tossed from side to side on top of her head every time she took a step.

"Does he realize he's supposed to be the first guest?" Nick asked sarcastically.

"I believe he does."

"Then get him back on the phone and find out where he is."

Seconds later she shouted, "He's on the Post Road across from Chipotle! There's an accident about 150 yards ahead of him."

"Tell him to make a U-turn, go back up the hill and turn left on Burr Street. Follow that all the way back down until it runs into the Merritt," and then almost as an afterthought he added under his breath, "and tell him to leave earlier next time if he wants us to push his book."

"I don't ha-ve tooo. He heard you, and says he will," Katy cooed.

One of the sound technicians boomed in over the loud speaker in the studio, "Um, Nick, we're not getting any sound from Barb's microphone."

Barbara Trower was the host of *Fairfield County Weekly*. She was a former affiliate news anchor in Orlando, and eventually a national news reporter for NBC in New York City, who quit after being passed over for an anchor position for the third time. She accepted the job at *FCW*, because it allowed her to act like the princess she no longer was, all within ten miles of the home she shared with her State Trooper husband of ten years. She had blonde, wavy hair, blue eyes and a nice, although slightly wooden smile, that was the result of a face-lift or two.

"Really Nick. Can't you get a more efficient sound crew? It's the same thing every week," Barb said.

"Check all the connections," Nick told a technician. "Then check the batteries. And make sure her microphone switch is on in the control room."

"That's it," came the response. "The switch wasn't on. Thanks, Nick."

Barb expressed her disgust with an eye roll and a shake of her head.

Four minutes before they took the air, Ben Weiner strolled into the studio. One minute after that, Barb spilled water down the front of her blouse and blamed the lighting technician for blinding her as the reason.

"Shit. Shit. Shit," she exclaimed.

"Do you have another blouse in your office?" Nick asked.

"No, I don't have another blouse!" she snapped. "I wasn't planning on the gaffer blinding me while I sipped my water."

Nick looked around the studio before his eyes settled on Katy. "Kate, would you mind?" he asked, motioning to her blouse.

"Oh great," Barb groaned. "I'll look like I'm wearing a nightgown."

"Not many options right now. You guys can change in my office. We've got two and a half minutes," he said, leading the way.

The two women undressed inside while Nick stood guard at the door.

"Nick. My hands are shaking. I need you to button up my blouse for me," Barb said, sticking her head out the door.

If he had time to think, he would have asked Katy to do it. Instead, he entered the room and fastened the buttons in very workman-like fashion, while Katy stood in her bra holding Barb's very wet blouse in front of her with her thumb and forefinger. Nick, who until that point, had been trying to avoid looking at Katy's very pleasing body, finally took notice once he had finished helping Barb.

"One minute til air, Nick," a voice shouted from outside the room.

"That's soaked, Kate. Here. Wear my shirt,"

he said as he quickly took his off and handed it to her.

"Nice muscles," Barb said with a smile, squeezing his right arm as she walked past.

Nick reappeared in the studio wearing only a white, cotton undershirt with his dress slacks and penny loafers. Katy followed a couple of moments later wearing his shirt, having had to roll the sleeves up five times before they came above her wrist.

"Good afternoon and welcome to Fairfield County Weekly, the show that brings you the best in local talent along with a sprinkling of national news. I'm Barb Trower, your host, and this week we bring you best selling self-help writer, Ben Weiner, author of Help Me, Help You, along with the country tinged musical styling's of The Musings."

"Thanks for the shirt," Katy whispered.

"You look better in it than I do," he answered. He had meant it more as a matter of fact than as a compliment, but she beamed from ear to ear nonetheless. "And don't listen to Barb's stupid comments. You saved the show."

"I understand," Katy said. "When I'm old, in a loveless marriage, and my looks are failing, I'm sure I'll be a bitch too."

Nick stifled a laugh and nudged her with his shoulder before walking back to the control room.

~

"You know she wants you," Katy stated while she helped Nick clean up after the show.

"Who wants me?"

"Barb."

"Are you on crack? Crack isn't good for a

college student."

"Crack is whack. I'm telling you. She wants you. She could have buttoned her blouse herself or asked me to do it, but she asked you. And I didn't see you hesitate much either."

"Because the show was starting in sixty seconds. I would have helped Queen Elizabeth button her blouse under those circumstances."

"Eww," Katy laughed. "Fine, but I'm telling you, she is all about you."

"She's been married for ten years to a good guy."

"A good guy who's probably never around, and who's probably cheating on her with some 25 year old he pulled over for a traffic stop."

"Every time I've seen them together, they seem very happy."

"That's because they're always drunk when you see them. Trust me on this one. Women can always spot another woman on the prowl."

"I trust you, Kate. But I still think you're crazy," Nick said as his phone beeped from an incoming text message.

Come out for a drink with us.

Nick froze just long enough for Katy to notice.

"It's from her, isn't it?!"

When he didn't answer, she knew she was right.

"What does she want?!"

"She wants me to go out for a drink."

"I told you!" Katy exclaimed gleefully.

"There are other people out with her as well. Want to go? Oh wait. You couldn't get into the bar," he said sarcastically.

"I'm 22 smartypants," she said, counting it

off for him by flashing her index and middle finger twice in a row. "Besides, I doubt they'd card me if I was with you. They'd think I was with my father."

"Touche."

"In all seriousness, I would love to go and watch her hit on you, but unfortunately, my sister's engagement party is tonight."

"That would be the sister you *didn't* set me up with?"

"I didn't know you then. And you better stay away from her, you homewrecker!" Katy warned.

"Stay away from who? Barb? Or your sister?" Nick smiled.

"BOTH."

"I'll see you Tuesday, Kate."

"Next week's my last week," she said. "And remember, you promised to buy me a drink on my birthday."

"I will."

Nick decided to go home and watch the Mets bullpen blow another game instead of meeting up with the others. At about nine o'clock, his doorbell shook him from a semi-conscious daze. He rubbed the sleep from his eyes, took an inordinately long time to walk the ten feet to the door and opened it; only to see a teary eyed Barb Trower standing before him.

"Barb? What's wrong?"

"I'm sorry to barge in on you like this," she said, entering without even waiting for him to ask her in.

"Don't you mean *Barb* in on me?" Nick responded, proud of his play on words. She didn't even pick up on it. He shrugged his shoulders as she pushed past him.

"I didn't know where else to go. I can't go to my mother's. She thinks I'm a selfish snob."

It was kind of hard to argue with her mother on that one.

"Did you and James get in a fight?"

"Not a fight. I just can't take it anymore. It's so—so....suffocating. When he was working the overnight shift it was better. We each did our own thing and would see each other on occasion. But now he's around all the time. I feel like I can't breathe."

"Um, I think that's called marriage," Nick offered quietly, trying unsuccessfully to find the balance between telling her what she wanted to hear and the truth.

"Do you have anything to drink?" she asked, as if he had never even spoken.

"Beer. Some water. Possibly a ginger ale."

"No hard liquor?"

"I don't really drink it."

"I wasn't asking for you."

"Right, well, since I don't really drink it, I don't really keep any here," he explained.

"Well, then I guess beer it is."

Nick fetched a couple of cold beers and returned to find Barb with her shoes off and Katy's blouse mostly undone.

"Make yourself comfortable," Nick said uncomfortably.

"I really can't stand this blouse any longer. That Katy is a sweet girl, but her perfume makes me want to vomit."

She took it off and tossed it onto the couch. Her body was nothing short of spectacular for a woman in her early forties. He hadn't really noticed earlier because he was too focused on the show. It was just as well, he thought. It would have been an unwelcome distraction.

"Let me get you a t-shirt or sweater or jacket or overcoat...something," he stammered.

"You don't have to," she said. "I'm comfortable."

"Well, I'm either going to have to get you a shirt or me a blindfold."

"You're like a 15 year old boy seeing his first semi-naked woman. It's cute."

She wasn't far off. It had been a while.

"Why does your mom think you're selfish?" he asked once he returned with a shirt. He was careful to sit more than an arm's length away, as if she was a viper that could lash out at any moment.

"She's just always loved James, and thinks I'm being mean."

"And what does James think?"

"I think if you were to ask him, he would say everything is fine."

"Sounds like the two of you need to talk."

"There's not really much to talk about. I can't go through another ten years. Life's too short."

"Isn't he wondering where you are right now?"

"Probably. But I don't care. There have been plenty of times where he stayed out all night with his fellow troopers."

"So you're not planning on going home?"

"Well, I guess that depends on you."

"I really don't see it as being a very good idea for you to stay here," Nick answered quickly, sliding even further away from her.

"Why not?"

"You're married for starters."

"I won't be forever."

"Plus, we work together."

"We're just friends. If Jerry came by here needing a place to stay, you'd let him wouldn't you?"

"I suppose."

"Then what's the difference?"

"Jerry wouldn't be wearing a sky lace push up bra."

"With a matching thong," she added with a wink.

"Look. Nothing good would come from you staying here. It certainly wouldn't help your marriage any. Don't get me wrong. I find you extremely attractive, but the bottom line is this; I wouldn't want anyone to cheat on me, so I certainly wouldn't want to do it to somebody else. I'm sorry."

"Why, Nick Nelson. You must be the last of the nice guys."

"I've been called worse," he said with a wry smile.

"I doubt that," she said as she kissed him on the cheek goodbye.

Once she had left, Nick picked up Katy's blouse from the couch and held it to his face in order to smell the perfume Barb hated so, and he immediately found himself overwhelmed by the two competing smells of heaven and hell.

V   THE CLOSER & THE BIG FISH

"It wasn't intentional. That's just how it worked out," Rick explained when Tom questioned his motives after he had lured the five youngest and prettiest secretaries from Pressman-Griggs over to their new firm.

It worked out because he had taken them all for drinks and told them what they wanted to hear. Casual dress on Fridays, followed by company sponsored happy hours. Instead of Executive Secretaries, they would be Assistant Executives with the opportunity to advance if they took the time to really learn the business. The clincher was when he promised box seats anytime Dave Matthews, John Mayer or Nelly rolled into Madison Square Garden.

What he didn't bother to explain to Tom was that the youngest secretaries usually worked for the oldest and most senior executives. They were the ones who knew all the secrets and usually had the most friends in the company. In fact, they were the ones that informed him Griggs was telling clients Rick was "on drugs" and they had to let him go. Griggs knew the other three weren't enough of a draw on their own to steal any major clients. But Rick was a threat and Griggs knew that it would only take one of the big clients to leave before the rest followed.

"I know you and Jane go way back," the man seated across the conference table said after Rick had flown all night to meet with him in person.

"We do in fact. We went to high school together."

"And I've always admired the work you've done for us."

"Thank you."

"But I'd be lying if I said I didn't have any concerns. I'm sure you know the rumors going around about you."

"Well, here's the thing about rumors," Rick responded, "If there was any truth to them, they'd be called facts instead."

"So you're saying I don't have anything to worry about?"

"That's exactly what I'm saying. Look, Jim, you've known me for more than ten years. And during that same time, you've gotten to know Bill Griggs as well, so it should be relatively easy for you to understand why he and I don't like each other. In the end, it was pretty simple. I grew tired of doing his work for him, so I left. There's nothing more to it than that."

"And if we came with you, we'd be leaving the most respected advertising firm in the world."

"And coming to a very good firm with a lower overhead, which will afford us the opportunity to take on fewer clients, which in turn, will enable us to provide more individual attention to the ones we do take on."

"But you won't have the same structure or support group that Pressman-Griggs has," the man continued. "I know Tom Reynolds is good, but I've never heard of Vossler and Jones."

"They were two of Pressman's finest young turks. Real up and comers," Rick explained.

"Our company is in too competitive a marketplace to be on the job training for young executives."

"Trust me. They're very talented. Besides, you and I both know that a team is only as good as its quarterback. If you come with us, you get me. If you stay with them, you get Bill Griggs."

The man didn't seem convinced.

"Let me put it this way," Rick began. "We're in San Francisco, so I'm assuming you're a 49ers fan."

"Of course."

"And you probably loved Joe Montana."

"Absolutely."

And when they let him go to the Chiefs toward the end of his career, you still rooted for him, didn't you?"

"Sure. But I didn't up and move to Kansas City," the man answered.

"And when the Niners played the Chiefs in that Monday Night football game, do you remember who won?"

The man smiled. "Montana."

"Exactly."

"But Steve Young led the Niners to the Super Bowl that same season."

For the briefest of moments, it appeared as though the best closer in the game, might have lost one.

"And they haven't won one in the fifteen years since, after winning four in nine years with Montana."

"What's your point?"

"My point is this. Pressman-Griggs will remain a strong firm. We're certainly not going to put them out of business. But they won't be nearly as strong without us. Even more important is the fact that you have the opportunity to sign Joe Montana. And not just for the last two years of his career. You have a chance to get him in his prime."

After what seemed to be an eternally long period of time, the man's scowl slowly evaporated into a slow smile. "Ok, Montana," he said, extending his hand, "We'll come with you. For now."

"You won't regret it," Rick assured him.

The man shook his hand. "I hope not."

Rick called Tom as soon as he stepped outside the building. "Del Monte's coming with us."

"Beautiful. What about Heineken and Champion?"

"Both with us."

"Sam Adams?"

"They're going to stay with them."

"By my count, that gives us nine clients. We wanted ten. Not bad."

"We'll have number ten within the hour. I'm on my way over to Facebook as we speak," Rick said, clicking his phone shut.

Facebook was an internet based communication company whose sole revenue was generated by advertising. Designed as a way for people to meet up with old friends, or new ones for friendship or relationships, its founder started it back when he was only a sophomore at Harvard. Since that time, he had turned down several billion dollar offers to sell the company outright, instead selling off only a 1.6% share of it to Microsoft. He was very hands-on, and it took Rick less than ten minutes to convince him that coming with a talented, small firm would provide the individual attention he was looking for.

When Rick's plane finally landed back in New York at well after two in the morning, he was so exhausted that he almost forgot to pay the cab driver when he dropped him off in front of his apartment building. He staggered to the front door, where he was greeted by the doorman.

"I'm sorry, Mr. McDermott, but I can't let you in," the man said.

"Very funny, Ronny. I'm so tired, I'm going to sleep until Wednesday."

"Not here you're not. You don't live here anymore."

"I'm not in the mood, Ronny," Rick said, trying to push past him.

"Pressman-Griggs owns the building. It's company housing, and although you paid the rent, your lease states that you have to be an employee to live here. They've packed up your things and sent them to storage. Here's the address and key to the storage facility."

Rick had always known that was the case, but it had been so long, he had forgotten until just now. "Look, Ronny, how bout letting me crash on the floor in there until morning?"

"I'm afraid I can't do that."

The man seemed to be enjoying himself a bit too much, but over the years, Rick knew he hadn't always treated him that well, so fair play to him. Payback was a bitch. He took the address and key from Ronny's open palm and left.

The first three hotels he tried were all full. His options were fairly limited. He could continue to search for a hotel with a vacancy, which would probably prove a fruitless effort, seeing as it was Easter Weekend. He could stay in a roach motel for nearly the same price. Or he could show up at the one place he knew he would be welcome in the middle of the night.

He got in his car and drove out to Connecticut, pulling into the arched, stone-cut driveway in front of the large white colonial down by the water. After ringing the doorbell, he heard some shuffling from within, followed by a light coming on. A bleary-eyed Nick Nelson opened the door, and stepped aside to let him enter without saying a word. There would be plenty of time for explanations in the morning.

VI   **THE TRUTH TELLER**

Rick poured a fresh cup of coffee as soon as he saw Nick descending the spiral staircase into the living room.

"So I assume you had just dropped your girlfriend off at Fairfield U last night and didn't feel like making the drive all the way to the city?" Nick asked after taking his first sip.

"I told you my girlfriend goes to Poquonac, and no. I returned from San Francisco only to find I had been evicted from my apartment."

"Evicted? What did you forget to pay your rent?"

"Nothing like that. Pressman-Griggs owns the building where I live, or I should say, where I *lived*. It's corporate housing, meaning I paid the rent, but the lease states that you need to be an employee to live there, which I clearly, no longer am. I'd just been living there so long, I completely forgot about it."

"I thought you had two or three other homes anyway."

"I do, but it would be a tough commute getting to New York City from Nantucket or Ft. Lauderdale."

"So what are you going to do?"

"I'll find a place this week," Rick said assuredly.

"Well, there's plenty of room here."

"I appreciate that. A couple of days would really help me out."

"Stay as long as you like. It'd be fun to have some company."

"Thanks, Nick. It's nice of you to take in someone you don't even know that well. I didn't know where else to turn. All my other friends are—"

Nick finished his sentence for him, "—married?"

"Well....yeah."

"No problem. Look, I've got to head into work for our prep day. Last episode before we go on a two month hiatus this weekend. Make yourself at home."

"Would it be ok if I tagged along? I wouldn't mind seeing exactly what it is you do," Rick said earnestly.

"Sure. C'mon in with me. But I have to warn you. It's not all that exciting."

Prep day was the day before filming where they checked equipment to make sure it was all running properly, confirmed guests, and edited together all video inserts. Nick introduced Rick around a bit before one of the digital editing computers crashed and he was summoned to the editing bay. It took Rick all of five minutes to then ferret out the available women, or at least those that would readily *make* themselves available on short notice.

"How bout that host of yours?" Rick said once he caught up to Nick.

"Barbara? What about her?"

"She's an attractive woman."

"Isn't she a bit old for you? She's 42."

"Well, I could always apply for an exemption."

"Apply? To whom? The He-Man Cradle Robbers Club?"

"That's pretty good. And yes, there actually is a club."

"Are you serious?"

"No, I'm not serious. It isn't a conscious thing. It's just sort of worked out that way. But I'm not adverse to seeing how the other half lives."

"Well, she's married."

"Perfect. She won't talk," Rick said as he went back over to join her.

"Who's the ass?" Katy asked once Rick was out of earshot.

"Just a friend of mine."

"He doesn't seem like he'd be a friend of yours."

"No? Why not?"

"Because he's not very nice."

"What makes you say that?"

"He told me if I swapped the glasses for a set of contacts, I wouldn't look like such a school marm."

"And what did you say?" Nick asked, amused.

"I told him if he didn't speak, he wouldn't sound like such an asshole."

Nick laughed loudly enough that he caught the attention of a handful of people at work in the studio. He loved Katy's no nonsense approach to life. She had no problem making fun of herself, but heaven help anyone else who did.

"He calls himself a truth teller," Nick said,

still laughing. "He's really not a bad guy once you get to know him."

"They said the same thing about Hitler."

"For the record. I like your glasses. They make your blue eyes seem even bigger."

"Well, thank you," she answered. "By the way, do you remember what today is?"

"April 21st?"

"And?"

"Friday?"

"And?" She was getting annoyed now.

"Oh yeah. Mets-Phillies tonight. Thanks for reminding me."

"You're an ass. I hate you too. You and your truth telling friend are like twins."

"I'm just kidding, Kate. Happy Birthday."

"Thank you. You still taking me out for a drink? Tomorrow is my last day, ya know."

"Sure if you'd like, but wouldn't you rather spend your birthday with your friends?"

"I can go out with them anytime. Where should we go?"

"Should we ask Rick to join us?" Nick asked, knowing full well what the response would be.

"Let's not, and say we forgot," Katy said with a wink as she walked away.

When the editing bay was fixed, and other near catastrophes had been averted, Nick relaxed for a few minutes and watched Rick McDermott with interest. He found it fascinating that people were drawn to Rick, both those that liked him as well as those that didn't. He surmised that the latter category treated him like a car wreck. You just had to see for yourself. Nick was actually the opposite. Very few people were drawn to him, but those that were, would love him for life.

Nick finally pulled him away from the crowd. "So, maestro, I'm taking Katy out for a drink for her birthday. You want to come?"

"The school marm?"

"Yes, she was really happy when you called her that."

"I didn't say she was ugly. I can't help it if I'm a truth teller."

"Yes, well, would you like to join us?"

"No thanks. I'm actually kind of jet-lagged from my trip. If it's ok, I'll just go back, relax and watch the Mets game."

"That's fine." Nick wasn't sure if he was relieved or disappointed. Part of him wanted to have Rick around for comic relief to push through any lags in the conversation. The other part wouldn't mind having Katy's attention to himself.

"Hey, buddy, you better take these," Rick said, thrusting two condoms into his hand.

"Why are you giving me condoms?!"

"Well, if you don't know the answer to that one, then you're in more trouble than I thought."

"She works for me. We're friends. I'm like her big brother."

"If you say so, but let me just tell you that no 22 year old spends her birthday with some guy 14 years older than her because they have a lot in common. She wants to go on all the rides at Nickyland."

"You're insane," Nick said, shaking his head. "I'll see you back at the house."

Katy chose a martini bar not far from the studio. It was packed with the Friday afternoon happy hour crowd of people that were either kicking off their weekend, or postponing the inevitable journey home to face the family and kids.

"I've always wanted to come in here," she said. "It looks like a different world from the outside. Like everyone in here is leading a better life than the rest of us."

"And now that you're here?"

"Well, I think I was wrong. You see the guy and the lady two tables behind us?"

"Yeah."

"They're having an affair. He told her he's planning on telling his wife when he gets home."

"You're a fellow eavesdropper!" Nick exclaimed joyfully, giving her the knuckles.

"You too?!" she exclaimed.

"Of course. The two women at the bar? Their boss is a pervert. Always making crude jokes in front of them. But the one wears low cut tops to work anyway, because he lets her take longer lunches when she does."

Katy roared. "The guy over there with the toss about hair, with the young girl who looks like she could be his daughter? He's her teacher."

"High school or college?"

"High school. He's telling her how difficult it is to look out at her in the middle of class without wanting to take her right there."

"Take her where?" Nick asked.

"*Take* her, Nick. As in 'have sex', 'make love', 'do the horizontal bop'. My god, what planet are you from?" she laughed.

"Sorrrry that I don't have a dirty mind!"

"It's cute. Somewhat Little House on the

Prarieish, but very cute."

"Are there no normal people left in the world?"

"These people are normal. They represent most of society. We're the abnormal ones."

"I'm beginning to agree with you," Nick said as the waitress brought another round of drinks. "I can't believe you're drinking a Martini? Shouldn't you be doing shots or something?"

"It's an Appletini. And gross. I'm not looking to vomit later."

"That's good to know."

"Can I have your olive?" she asked.

"Sure," he said, holding it out on its stir stick for her.

She tossed it high into the air and caught it in her mouth with a smile. Nick loved how she could inject life into the stuffiest of places.

"Nice shot. Of course it's easier if you have a big mouth."

"Shut up."

"The truth hurts."

"Oh, I'm sorry. I thought I was out with Nick Nelson, not Rick the Dick."

"Fair enough," Nick laughed. "I'm going to miss you," he then added somewhat awkwardly.

"A compliment? I like those. They're so rare."

"In all seriousness, you did a great job for us. Your mother was so proud when she came to watch the taping last week."

"I doubt that. Nothing I ever do is good enough. My attitude isn't good enough. My grades aren't good enough. I spend half my life driving my little sister around, and instead of getting a thank you, I get yelled at because my sister will tell her I drove too fast."

"That's just your mom's way of making sure you stay her little girl."

"She's just so annoying."

"So, how are things with your boyfriend?" Nick asked. "I haven't seen him around the set in a while."

"That's because we broke up."

"Open mouth. Insert foot. Sorry about that."

"Don't be. He was getting on my nerves."

"How so?"

"He'd rather sit around playing X Box with his friends than just about anything else I can think of. College guys are so immature."

"I wish I could tell you it's limited to college guys, but unfortunately, it doesn't change much as they get older."

"You seem mature enough."

"That's because I'm a loser. Given the opportunity, I'd be just like the rest of them."

"You're not a loser," she laughed at his self-deprecating humor. What she didn't realize was that to a certain extent, he actually believed that about himself.

"It's just as well you broke up anyway."

"And why is that?"

"Because you're not going to marry your college boyfriend."

"Why not?"

"Because he's a placeholder," Nick responded.

"A placeholder?"

"Yeah. Until someone better comes along."

"Oh really?"

"I'm serious. Out of the literally thousands of people I know, exactly *one* has married their college girlfriend."

"You have thousands of friends. You must be so popular," she mocked.

"I didn't say I had thousands of friends. I said I *knew* thousands of people," Nick corrected.

"I'm only teasin. And only one, huh?"

"Just one."

"Well, then I'm glad we broke up," she said. "Time to start looking for Mr. Right."

"It's when you're not looking that you'll find him."

"Boy, you are full of wisdom tonight. Confucius say he should be tall, dark and handsome."

"Well, at least I'm tallish," Nick laughed.

"And sweet. And funny."

"Those qualities will get me a phone call at a pay phone," he said, only half joking.

"Those qualities are what make you adorable," she answered.

It was a case of the words coming out of her mouth before she could stop them. Maybe it was the Appletini talking, but Katy turned an embarrassed shade of red after she impulsively kissed him on the cheek.

For some unknown reason Nick had not yet worked out, the kiss, although innocent in nature, would rate highly on his list of favorite moments, right up there with the '86 World Series, scoring the winning run in a high school baseball game, and watching the first-ever episode of *Fairfield County Weekly* with friends. Most people's list also included losing their virginity, but that night was such a muddled mess with the school slut in the back of the auditorium that he preferred not to think about it.

~

He found Rick half-asleep when he returned, the TV much louder than one might rightfully need to have it. It was the first time he ever had seen him with his guard slightly down.

"Hey, the Mets won," he said, sitting up now.

"I heard," Nick answered. "Can I ask you something seeing as you're the resident expert in this area and all?"

"In what area?"

"Dating a younger woman."

"Sure."

"How do you do it?"

"Do what?"

"Date them."

"Pretty easily actually. They like guys with money who can make them laugh, and I like girls with tight bodies that aren't complicated."

"But what do you talk about with them? Do you ever run out of things to say?"

"I see where we're headed with this," Rick said, his sharpness having returned. "You had a good time with the school marm, but she's not going to be working there anymore so you're wondering how you can ask her out without coming across as a dirty old man, and also if you'll still have anything in common if you do go out."

He pretty much had pounded the nail into the hole with his assessment of the situation.

"Yeah."

"First of all, one thing I can spot is a young

woman who is attracted to an older guy. It's a look they have."

He pursed his lips together and opened his eyes wide in a ridiculous attempt to demonstrate what he meant. Nick burst into laughter.

"Laugh all you want, but it's true. Let me guess. She just broke up with her boyfriend because he's immature. He'd rather hang out with his buddies drinking or playing video games. So she's looking for someone to give her attention. Someone she respects. Someone she trusts won't screw her over. How am I doin so far?"

"Scarily good."

"She clearly likes you. I could tell that from the moment I first saw her around you. So call her up. If it makes you feel like less of a dirtbag, make up some bullshit excuse about how you want her opinion on what direction to take the show when it returns from hiatus. She'll say yes. You guys will have a few drinks, realize you miss each other, and then you'll end up banging the headboard against the wall for a few hours. It's perfect."

"And then what?"

"I'm not sure I follow what you're asking."

"Well, after that, then what? I mean, you date them. Do you have anything in common with them after you've done that? What do you talk about?"

"Oh, I see. Well, yes, technically, I do date them—for a while. We talk about sports, Lil Wayne, and *MTV* and then she'll go on and on about some friend of hers who's in a fight with her boyfriend because she caught him chatting up some freshman girl in the quad, that he claims is the little sister of a friend of his. I don't know. I pretty much tune her out at that point."

"But what about long term? Can it work?"

"In a word, no. I mean, she can come over to your house anytime, but you can't exactly sleep in a college dorm room with her 200 pound roommate in the next bed five feet away. And you're not going to go to a Screw Your Roommate dance with four hundred 18-22 year olds. Trust me, I've done it. It's fun once, but the hangover the next day isn't worth it."

"She's graduating in a couple of weeks so it's a little different."

"Yes and no. Eventually you'll get tired of always going out and she'll get tired of not having a normal relationship, and go back to some idiot her age, so they can go club hopping and hang out at the beach. But if you're looking for some great sex, and the opportunity to have your guy friends drool when you bring her around, while your female ones foam at the mouth from jealousy, then I highly recommend it. But I would brush up on back episodes of *Pretty Little Liars* and *The Bachelorette* first."

"So, it can't really work."

"For you, no. You're the last of the nice guys, Nick. You'd feel guilty all the time, and then she'd break your heart when she left you. Me? I'm shallow and self-absorbed. I don't care so much about that as long as the sex is good. And they all leave eventually. Trust me on that. Of course they always come back a few years later, but by then I've usually moved on to their friend's younger sister or something."

Nick nodded. It was exactly what he needed to hear. Unfortunately, in life's version of rock, paper, scissors, the heart trumped the brain every time.

VII   SHAMELESS

*T*he weeks that followed the taping of the last show of the season were for Nick, a harmonious melody of exercise, yard work and relaxing days at the beach, save for one horrific experience where he accidently stumbled upon a leather skinned, 65 year old woman sunbathing topless.   It was a memory that would be forever burned into his psyche, but after three days in bed, he was finally coaxed back out into the world.

In the meantime, Rick remained at his house, his three day stay having been extended to the better part of a month, in part because it was easy, and Rick always did what was easy, but also because Nick never pushed for him to leave.   He liked having someone to go the Mets games with and watch Monday Night Football at the local pub.   He liked the Sunday morning softball and flag football games followed by margaritas at an outdoor patio bar.   But most of all, he liked the company.   For the first time in his life, he felt like he was running with the popular crowd.

Following his conversation with Rick, he decided against calling Katy, because he wondered how he could take advice from someone whose longest standing relationship was with a pair of boxers. Rick's most recent relationship had ended as he predicted, when his girlfriend left him for a boy much closer to her age and he mourned its end—for approximately three hours before he knocked on Nick's bedroom door one morning.

"Hey, buddy," he said, sticking his head just inside the door. "I've got a favor to ask."

When Nick didn't respond because he remained half-asleep, he continued. "I've got some company here, if you know what I mean, and I'm supposed to meet Tom in Manhattan in 45 minutes, so I don't really have time to get her back to campus. So, I was wondering if you would drop her off for me?"

"You're back with Joely?" Nick asked, sitting up now.

"Not exactly."

"Who then?"

"Her roommate," Rick winced, more because he knew what Nick reaction would be than because he was embarrassed.

"Oh.....my.....god. And you're dating her?!"

"Not sure you can call it dating. She's more of a slampiece if you will."

"Have you no shame whatsoever?!"

"Apparently not. But she's blazin."

"So let me get this straight. You would like me to drive home your college going one-night stand, who happens to be the roommate of your ex-girlfriend. Is that correct?"

"That pretty much covers it. If you can't, I'll put her in a cab, but I don't want to be an asshole or anything."

"Would you like me to buy her breakfast as well?"

"If you're not in a rush," Rick said. "As long as she makes her 10:30 class. Thanks, buddy. I owe you one."

"One hundred, maybe," Nick grumbled.

"I'll see you over at the studio this afternoon. Three o'clock right?"

"Three o'clock will be fine."

~

In a city of nearly eight million people, it made perfect sense that the place Tom and Rick chose to meet for breakfast was the same place that Bill Griggs had decided on. They hadn't seen him since the day they had been escorted from the building.

"You aren't going to go over there and make a scene, are you?" Tom pleaded.

"Doesn't look like I'll have to. He's on his way over here."

With Griggs was a younger, similarly dressed man.

"Bill. Larry," Tom nodded.

"Hi boys, how's The Mom and Pop Agency?" Griggs asked smugly.

"How's it feel to be the Captain of the Titanic?" Rick answered.

"Please. We're stronger than ever."

"That's funny because Tom and I had a bet when we left as to how many of your clients that we actually wanted, would stay with you. I said zero. I won."

"Oh, so you didn't want Sam Adams?"

Rick looked for a brief instant as if Griggs had a valid point, until, "Not once we signed Heineken. We thought it might be a conflict of interest."

"You guys don't even have your own production team or studio. It's only a matter of time before all your clients return to the big leagues."

"Yeah," Larry added, smacking the folded newspaper he was holding into Rick's chest, "then you'll be looking for jobs. The Want Ads are in the back of section C. Happy hunting."

"See you at the Chloe's boys," Griggs said with a laugh.

"Oh they invited you guys to come as seat fillers while we accept our awards?" Rick asked. "I'll be sure and fart in mine before I get up."

"That was mature," Tom said sarcastically once they had left.

"Tell me about it. A few years ago, I might have said something rude," Rick answered. He unfolded the paper Larry had left with him, and taped to the inside of it was a small, digital mini cassette.

"What's that?" Tom asked.

"You don't want to know."

"If I didn't want to know, I wouldn't have asked."

"Treat it like a mirage. You thought you saw something, but you really didn't."

"Uh huh," Tom nodded, thinking that where Rick was concerned, it was sometimes better to be left in the dark.

Meanwhile, in Connecticut, Nick had just finished eating breakfast at a local diner with Rick's one-night stand. He was amazed at how completely unaffected she seemed by the fact that she was being driven back to campus by a much older man, who she hadn't slept with the night before. He assumed it wasn't the first time.

"Thanks for breakfast and the ride," the girl said as he pulled into the circle in the center of campus.

"It's not a problem."

"Maybe I'll see you around," she added.

She hugged the first boy she saw once she exited the car, and Nick found himself both repulsed and impressed at the same time. As he began to pull away, he noticed Katy on the sidewalk having just witnessed him dropping the girl off. He quickly threw the car into park and jumped out.

"Hi, Kate. How are you?"

"Apparently I was wrong. You and your friend are more alike than I thought," she said with equal parts disappointment and disdain as she walked away.

"Kate, it's not what it looks like."

She didn't stop. He found himself now faced with the awkward decision of chasing her down the sidewalk with no guarantee she would even stop if he caught up with her, or leaving with what remained of his dignity. He chose the latter.

~

"I saw Katy when I dropped off your 'slampiece' this morning. She seemed pretty upset. She obviously got the wrong idea," he explained to Rick when they met up later in the day.

"That's good."

"What exactly is good about it?"

"It means she cares. Plus, it now gives you a reason to call her. So do that, while I'm putting this public service announcement together. Thanks for letting me into the editing bay."

"What's the PSA for?"

"Good hygiene." Nick answered.

"Can I see it?"

"I'll let you see it when it's done."

"Ok, well, I'll be in my office."

"Call her."

By the time Rick knocked on his office door an hour and a half later, Nick had opened and closed his cell phone at least a dozen times, without actually dialing a number.

"Did you call her?" Rick asked.

"Not exactly."

"You are so full of shit."

"Excuse me?"

"You want to fall in love, but you're not willing to do anything to make that happen."

"I didn't think you could make that happen. I thought it did or it didn't. Besides, you were the one who told me it would never work out with her."

"It won't. But sometimes you have to throw yourself in front of the bus."

"Have you ever thrown yourself in front of a bus?"

"I'm not a romantic. Let me ask you something. Have you ever even been in love?"

"There was this girl in college from Alaska. She was half Irish and half Eskimo. My friends used to call her Nanook of the North. She was actually the roommate of a friend of mine. So one Easter break, I decided to stay up at school rather than driving a long ways for just a couple of days. Jami, that was my friend, told me I should call her roommate up because she wasn't going home either. So I did. We went to dinner one night and it was the strangest thing. Everything she thought, I thought. Everything she said, I was about to say. We had so many things in common, it was spooky. And not things like we both liked spaghetti or donuts. Strange things like obscure movies, and the fact that neither of us liked to eat food we had to battle with, like lobster, watermelon or any food with seeds or pits. Anyway, I called her after I dropped her off that night, and she and I stayed on the phone until sunrise. The next day, everyone returned from break, and Jami made it clear she didn't want me dating her roommate, even though she and I were just friends."

"Typical female. Even though she might not have wanted to date you, she was going to make damn sure no one else did either, because she wanted all of your attention. So what did you do?"

"I backed off."

"Why?!"

"I didn't see the point. She was never going to leave Alaska, and as much as I wanted to visit, I wasn't about to move there."

"That's what I mean. You give up too easily."

Nick didn't answer because he knew Rick was right.

"So that's it? Just that one girl?"

"There was one other girl. I met her on a trip to Europe. She was from Cincinnati. Melanie Petrovsky was the first girl who ever made me realize that personality is what made a girl beautiful."

"What a ridiculous thought."

"I'm serious," Nick said. "Don't get me wrong. She was cute. But more than that, she was smart, and funny, and sweet, and innocent. We ended up trapped in a hot, sweaty, cramped elevator in Florence with ten complete strangers for more than three hours and I didn't even care. And I'm claustrophobic."

"Of course you are. So what happened?"

"The distance was a bit much. Eventually the calls and visits became less frequent. But every time we did speak, it was as if we had spoken only the day before."

"When's the last time you spoke to her?"

"About ten years ago. Right before she became an actress."

"She's an actress? Been in anything I would know?"

"Pretty sure," Nick nodded. "Melanie Price?"

"You know Melanie Price?!"

"Uh, huh."

"And you haven't called her because..."

"She's a movie star. And she's engaged."

"To that idiot from that boring English movie that won a couple of Academy Awards a few years back. The guy is like 60," Rick exclaimed.

"Look who's talking? You're dating a 20 year old."

"That's different. I'm not 60."

"Who are you trying to kid? You'll still be dating 20 year olds when you're 60."

"I don't know about that, but I like where your mind is at. In all seriousness, why don't you call her? Call Katy. Call someone for God's sake," Rick said, exasperated, shaking his head, "before you end up...."

"Before I end up--?"

"Like me," he said simply. It was first sign of vulnerability Rick had shown in the time he had known him.   "I'll see you back at the house."

Nick sat motionless for a moment once Rick had left before dialing a number on his cell phone. Katy answered on the third ring. He hit the *end* button and dropped the phone on his desk. Calling was the first step. He would work on speaking another time.

VIII   A TROOPER, A PAN, & A ROAD TRIP

Nick loved being up and about in the early morning hours almost as much as he hated the actual act of waking up. And it didn't matter if it was sunny or overcast; breezy or still. Being awake at sunrise made him feel as though he had gained an advantage over all those that remained lying in their beds. Waking up on this day, however, was easier than most as he hadn't slept much the night before.   Rick's words had caromed around his head most of the night, like a pinball bounding off bumpers and walls in desperate search of a resting place.

Before you end up like me.

What was so awful about being Rick McDermott?   After all, he was good-looking, intelligent, athletic, charming in his own gruff, sarcastic way, and nearly always in the company of an attractive younger woman. He was also successful, and Nick had known plenty of people with all of the above qualities who weren't.   Where the younger women were concerned, it could be viewed one of two ways. Either he had the ability to relate to people of all ages, or he was a real-life Peter Pan—forever young, and refusing to get any older.

Either way, he could think of worse lives to lead. He had wanted to ask him what he meant when he said that, but knew Rick would have tried to deflect it with humor or a throw away sarcastic comment. If he was going to ever fully understand Rick McDermott, he was going to have to figure him out for himself.

This morning was an early spring day that acted like a pre-cursor to a late one—sunny skies and a light breeze—the first day that didn't require a sweatshirt for his morning walk. He knew there would be cool days still to come, but for now he enjoyed it. There was something uplifting about the first nice day of spring.

He had scarcely walked through the front door when Rick thrust a piece of paper into his hand.

"What's this?"

"It's a present."

"Doesn't look like much of a present."

"Read it."

"121 North Adams Street. Chicago. What is this?"

"The address where Melanie Price's new movie is being filmed."

"What?! How?"

"How is not important. Besides, that's not the present," Rick exclaimed. "The present is that we're going to take a little road trip to see her."

"There is no way I am going to do that."

"You have no reason not to. You're on vacation for three more weeks. I could use a little one myself. We can even catch a Cubs game while we're there. They're filming on the north side, not five minutes from Wrigley Field."

"She's engaged."

"So? She's not married yet. If the Mets are trailing going into the 9th inning, do they just end the game?"

"They might as well. They usually lose."

"But on those rare occasions when they don't, it's glorious."

"I'm not a spontaneous person. I don't do things that don't make sense."

"And I'm irrational. I do things like this all the time. So let's compromise."

"What's the compromise?"

"We go to Chicago to see her."

"Where's the compromise in that?"

"I won't make you buy an engagement ring until you've actually spoken to her again."

"Some compromise."

"I'm kidding. Look, what's the worst thing that happens? You see her, maybe go to lunch. If you don't hit it off, you leave, she gets married and you return to your miserable lonely life in Connecticut."

His heart, which for some unknown reason held out some faint hope that this might actually work, was grappling with his brain, which knew in no uncertain terms that it wouldn't. In the end, he decided if he was going to ever truly get to know Rick McDermott, there would no better opportunity than this.

"When would we leave?"

"Day after tomorrow. I have to tie up a few loose ends first."

The loose ends Rick needed to tie up kept him out of the house into the evening, the solitude only serving to make Nick question whether going on the trip was really the right decision. In the short time he had known her, Katy had become the person he usually turned to in times of uncertainty. She seemingly always was able to provide clarity in times of confusion, but he couldn't call her now. She was not happy with him, and this frivolous journey he was about to embark on would only make things worse.

He cracked open a beer and settled in front of the television with a Salisbury Steak Hungry Man dinner at about seven-thirty. He was asleep about forty-five minutes later, only to be awakened by the doorbell.

Nick was still somewhat groggy, or he would have certainly looked through the peephole before opening it at that time of night. He figured Rick had probably forgotten his key. Besides, what criminal rang the doorbell before entering?

He hadn't even opened it halfway when it was pushed open from the other side with the brute force of a man shoving him backwards into his living room. Barbara Trower's husband would have been menacing even if he hadn't been brandishing the business end of his state-issued nine millimeter in Nick's face.

"So you think it's ok to fuck around with other people's wives?!" he growled.

"I have no idea what you're talking about," Nick responded in a panic.

"I followed her a few nights ago, and she came here."

If Nick had been thinking more clearly, he would have asked which night, and tried to eliminate himself as a suspect by proving he was elsewhere. But the only thing he could think of was that the night he was referring to was the night she had shown up. If he had known this would be the end result, he would have slept with her. Actually, that wasn't true. He probably wouldn't have anyway. Far better to die a noble death.

"She stopped by after she had a few drinks with other people from the show. I didn't even go. She said the two of you got in a fight and she didn't want to go home right away. We talked for a few minutes, but that was it. And I haven't seen or heard from her since."

"Shut the hell up," Jay Trower answered, the pupils of his eyes so low in their sockets that they were now barely visible.

"Ask her. I'm sure she'll tell you the same thing," Nick said, wondering if she really would.

"I don't believe a word that cheating whore says!"

Sanity had clearly left the building.

Just then there was a barely audible click at the back door, so quiet that it could have been confused with a washing machine, refrigerator or the central air turning on.

"What's going on here?" Rick asked, dropping his bag on a chair.

Nick was never so happy to see anyone in his entire life, but wondered why he hadn't called 9-1-1. Maybe he had and was just trying to buy some time.

"Who the hell are you?!" Jay said.

"He's my roommate," Nick answered. "Rick, this is Jay Trower. I don't know if you remember Barbara from the show?"

"What seems to be the problem, Jay?"

"This asshole is fucking my wife."

"What makes you think that?"

"He just is."

"Look, I don't know your wife very well, but I know this much. If she's having an affair with someone, it certainly isn't with Nick. It took him four years to bang his high school girlfriend."

It was somewhat of a backhanded compliment, Nick thought to himself with an internal shrug.

"I know she was over here."

"Maybe it had something to do with work? And even if it didn't, cheating isn't the cause of a marriage ending. It's a symptom that something else is wrong." Even Rick seemed to be having his doubts about Nick now.

"I don't care what the reason is."

"So you're just going to kill him, without any proof that something happened?!"

Nick didn't like the fact that Rick was giving him suggestions. How fitting that he was about to be shot for something he didn't even do. It would undoubtedly end up splashed all over the morning papers, and he would be vilified in death. What bothered him most was all the times where he had done the right thing instead of the fun thing. If people were going to hate him, he wished he would have at least had the benefit of the pleasure.

"I don't need any more proof."

Rick nodded. "Panhead," he said.

"What?!" Jay screamed.

"Panhead," Rick repeated.

"What the hell is he talking about?" Jay asked, turning to Nick for answers.

"I have no idea," Nick said, pretty much

resigned to his fate at that point.

The split second Jay turned to Nick was all that Rick needed to reach over the counter and grab the skillet in which he had made scrambled eggs that morning. With a compact homerun hitter's swing, he smashed the trooper across the side of his head, rendering him a useless heap on the floor.

"Pan," Rick said, holding up the skillet, "Head," he continued, pointing to the man's head.

"What do we do now? You do realize he's a state trooper."

"In that case, I suggest we think about leaving on our trip a little early."

The words were not very consoling.

"I'm kidding," Rick said. "Do you have any rope?"

"Rope?"

"Relax. We're not going to hang him. We're just going to restrain him a little while we talk some sense into him."

They tied him to a chair and waited for him to come to. When he did, Rick handed him four Tylenol, an icepack and a glass of water.

"Now, we can do this the easy way, or the hard way," he said. "The easy way is you apologize to my friend here for falsely accusing him and leave quietly, never to return or even look at him at an office party or for any other reason. The hard way is I'll call another friend, who happens to be the Commissioner of Public Safety for the State of Connecticut and you'll be out of a job by sunrise with no pension to boot."

Jay was still a bit groggy. "I'm sorry," he mumbled. "I lost it."

"It's ok," Nick responded, more relieved than anything. "I hope it works out for you."

The man slowly and somewhat unsteadily walked from the house holding an ice pack to the side of his head. It was hard not to feel a little sorry for him.

"Wow," Nick said.

"No kidding."

"You do believe that nothing happened when she was here, don't you?"

"Of course I do."

"Good. I wasn't sure for a minute there. Can you believe that? That was crazy."

"I know. Especially when I'm the one who slept with her," Rick answered matter of factly.

IX   THE WORLD ACCORDING TO RICK

Rick is behind the wheel. Nick is sprawled comfortably in the passenger seat of Rick's Maserati.

"I can't believe you have a Maserati," Nick said. "What are they, like two hundred grand?"

"Not quite. And you have a Porsche, so what the hell are you talking about?"

"A Porsche is a poor man's Maserati."

"Oh, please. And while we're on the subject, come clean. Where did you get your money? Inherit it? Steal it? Deal coke on the side? Run a prostitution ring?"

"None of the above," Nick laughed and hesitated before relenting. "Ok. Here it is, and if you tell anyone, I will kill you."

He had Rick's full attention now. "I'm listening."

"I made a bunch of money when I sold my first house. Its value tripled because of its location by the train station. But I've also made a big chunk of money playing blackjack at the casino."

"Excuse me?"

"Blackjack," Nick repeated.

"What are you, Rain Man?"

"Let's just say I learned to count cards."

"How do you *learn* to count cards?"

"Practice. You give values to each card and count through multiple decks as quickly as you can. I can pretty much count every card in a hand within ten seconds."

"So you always win? You're like a sure thing?"

"Not always. You could know the *exact* card about to come out and still lose the hand. Sometimes, you're just going to lose. But...I've won more than I've lost. Much more."

"Why don't you just quit your job and play Blackjack full time?"

"Because I'm sure eventually they will come up with measures to prevent it from happening. They already have in some places. Cut further into the decks. Automatic shuffle machines. Single deck with the cards face down..."

"That's awesome. Guess where we're headed when we get back?"

"Please don't say anything to anyone," Nick pleaded.

"Fine. I won't. But we're still going when we get back."

They drove on quietly for a few minutes before Nick broke the silence. "I can't believe you slept with Barb Trower," he said at last.

"I didn't have to tell you, you know. You would have never known. Anyway, here's what I think. I think you should leave the show and come work with us. Full partner."

"Doing what? I don't know the first thing about advertising."

"You'd be in charge of production. Produce and direct all of our ads."

"Do you even have a studio?"

"We're renting for the time being, but we will be building one."

"I don't know."

"What's not to know? It would be something different. You'd be working with friends. More flexible hours. Not to mention getting a big pay increase. Not that that matters to you, Rockafeller."

"I'm not that rich."

"*That* being the key word." Rick looked ahead and didn't like what he saw. "What the hell?"

Traffic had come to a screeching halt on the highway.

"Beautiful sunny day in the middle of the afternoon on a wide open road with no sign of construction and traffic is stopped cold."

"Must be an accident," Nick offered.

"Well, somebody better be dead or at least have multiple internal injuries if they're going to screw up our day like this. Drive straight. Look over your shoulder and use your turn signal before changing lanes. How difficult is that? Idiots."

"Don't sugar coat it. Tell me how you really feel. Anything else bothering you?"

Rick pointed at a car stopped in the next lane over.

"As a matter of fact, *that* bothers me," he said.

"What about it?"

"It's a Honda."

"And your point is?"

"It's a Honda with tinted windows, a low rider kit, the full chrome package, mag wheels, with dual exhaust and a whale tail. With all the extras, the freakin car probably cost 50K. So why not just buy a Mercedes?"

"Maybe he didn't want a Mercedes?"

"Listen. You can dress a chimp in a tuxedo, but it won't make him Brad Pitt."

Nick has no choice but to shake his head and laugh at the world according to Rick. The news on the radio interrupted their conversation.

"Details on the motive for the tragic shootings in Binghamton are finally becoming more clear as authorities found a letter stating how the gunman was upset over losing his job and with people ridiculing him for struggling to speak the English language..." the announcer stated.

"See? Now, this is what I don't get. The guy's pissed he lost his job and because people made fun of the way he speaks, so he goes into an ESL class and mows down 14 people, most of whom were probably no better off than he was! I mean, go into Yale and blow away an English professor or BIC and gun down the CEO. *That*, would at least make sense. It would be awful, but it would make sense. And then, the guy kills himself! If he wanted to do that, he should have just done that. Why take innocent people with him?! They should hire me as a Police Negotiator. I'd tell the guy, "Listen, if you want to kill yourself—DO IT. Put the barrel of the gun inside your mouth and pull the trigger, you useless piece of shit. DO IT. You don't need to take anybody else with you. Be a man and just kill YOURSELF, you big pussy."

"I think it's safe to say that you would be the worst Police Negotiator in history," Nick said, shaking his head.

X   MIDDLE AMERICA

Ten hours of driving left them somewhere in the middle of Ohio with another three or four hours to Chicago. They stopped for the night at the only hotel they could find for miles around. It was not exactly the Ritz Carlton, with its rusted out railings, and rooms that opened to a parking lot that shared space with a truck stop. They pulled around the side of the building to park and found two truckers drinking 40 ouncers in brown paper bags standing in the only open space in the entire lot.

"Get a load of these guys," Rick said.

The men were clad in plaid, flannel shirts with dirty wife beaters underneath; stained jeans, and hunting caps complete with the earflaps. They leered at the Maserati that was attempting to pull into the parking space they were standing in. It might as well have been a space ship to them.

"Is that there one of them Maze-r-eighties?" Rick mocked. "You know, Bud, it would be great ta drive that vee-hickel in tha next road rally. Then we could go off inta da woods and hunt us some pheasant. Course, we'd need to hook up a gun rack on the roof first."

"They're not moving. Why don't we just park somewhere else?" Nick said in a slight panic.

"Because there *is* nowhere else to park."

Rick lowered his window and leaned his head out. "Excuse us."

The man Rick had addressed continued to sip his beer. "Spot's taken."

Rick continued to pull forward unfazed, a slight nod of his head the only perceptible indication that he had actually heard the man. "Spot. For to park. Bar. To drink," Rick said.

"He *said*," the other man answered, raising his voice, "spot's *taken*."

Rick smiled and waved this time, but didn't stop. He continued forward, pinning the first man against a parking pole.

"You must not hear so good," the second man said as he started toward the car.

Rick threw open the door at that point, *smashing* him with the door, and sending him reeling backwards. Rick advanced quickly towards him and stood over him with his foot firmly planted on his chest. "Did you say something?"

"You have no idear who you're messin with."

"Based on how you look and what you're wearing, I'd say the first and second place finishers in the log rolling contest at the Special Olympics. Now, listen to me closely. As much fun as it probably is to sit in the Motel 6 parking lot, drinking bad beer in thirty-five degree weather, why don't you go home to your wives and compare who has the bigger gaps between their teeth?"

Rick let the guy stagger to his feet and motioned to Nick, who was now in the driver's seat, to back the car up enough to let the other man wriggle free. Both men looked as though they wanted to fight, but weren't sure what to make of Rick. Crazy had a way of intimidating even the surest of people. They chose to back away grumbling instead.

"What are the chances of the car still being here in the morning?" Nick asked as they made their way toward the lobby.

Rick pulled out his IPhone. "Better than average," he said. He called 9-1-1. "Hello. I'm calling from the Motel 6 in Toledo. There's a couple of drunk truckers in the parking lot harassing guests. Could you send someone over?"

~

The only light inside their hotel room soon came from the TV. Both Rick and Nick were asleep within minutes of their heads hitting the pillows when they were awakened by the sound of shattering glass outside.

"You might have wanted to specify sending out a cop who *wasn't* related to the truckers," Nick said, pulling back the curtain. Rick joined him at the window in time to see a police officer smash in the headlights on his car with a nightstick, while his partner took out the driver's side window. The truckers continued drinking their forty ouncers in the background while this was going on.

"Now what?" Nick asked.

"Not much we can do," Rick answered as he climbed back into his bed.

There was an eerie calmness with which he answered that made Nick wonder what was going through his mind. When Nick awoke a few hours later to find that Rick had already cleaned the glass from the driver's seat and affixed a piece of plastic over the empty window, he grew even more suspicious. But Rick never said a word. Not even when they pulled into the diner across the street to grab some breakfast. They sat in a side booth with a window view of the truck stop in silence. The trip had gotten off to a rough start.

Nick broke the silence at last. "I can't believe we're going to let those guys get away with what they did."

Rick broke off a piece of his coffee roll as he glanced at a truck across the street. "Sometimes, you need to let nature run its course."

"There they are!" Nick pointed. "I think they slept in their clothes.

Rick nodded with what appeared to be little more than a casual interest as he slowly chewed a bite of his omelet. The men pulled themselves up into the truck's cab and turned over the engine with a roar. The wheels suddenly began to spin as the truck strained to pull away. Something wasn't letting it. A closer look revealed a chain attached to the rear gate of the truck; the other end attached to a cement post in the parking lot. A second chain was attached to the rear chassis. There was a creaking sound, followed by the gate *catapulting* through the air. It landed on the cover of the nearby outdoor pool of the motel. What followed was a horrific crunching noise as the back undercarriage ripped apart. All four of the back wheels fell off in opposite directions from each other as the truck lurched forward, bouncing down the road, sending what was left of it, rearing upwards like a runaway colt. The tilt sent hundreds of bags of dry dog food pouring out onto the ground. As some of them ripped open, kibbles were strewn across the street like marbles in a six year old's playroom.

Nick's eyes grew wide as saucers. He looked at Rick. Then at the truck. Then back at Rick. "Nature?" he asked.

"You never can tell what it's going to do," Rick smiled, before adding with only the slightest sense of urgency, "We might want to get going now."

XI   THE SEARCH BEGINS

It took four hours of driving and a stop at a Chicago-area Maserati dealership before they could continue with their quest. The service manager questioned whether the damage to the car was the result of some heavy drinking the night before and gave him a 3-5 day time frame to fix it, but when Rick pulled out a stack of hundred dollar bills that could have filled the better part of a shoebox, the time frame changed to 24 hours and they were given a loaner car to head to 121 North Adams Street.

The home was a well-kept, two-story brownstone on the city's north side. It had no real yard to speak of and parking was limited to the street. Potted plants hung just outside the windows, adding what seemed like a female's touch to the place.

"What do we do now?" Nick asked, still not fully on board with the idea even though they had just pulled directly across the street from the movie set. There had to be a thousand people clamoring around trying to get a glimpse of one of the stars.

"We talk our way onto the set," Rick responded, with a nod toward the oversized security guard at the entrance to the set. He had a baby-face on top of a young, hulking figure that had muscles bulging out of an undersized t-shirt.

"We drive 1,000 miles to see someone I haven't seen in more than 20 years, who just happens to be engaged to be married, and that's your great plan?"

"You're looking at this all wrong."

"Enlighten me then, oh enlightened one."

"Look, you want nothing more than to find a wife and have a family. She's engaged. Which means she's open to the idea."

"Are you insane? She's engaged to *someone else!*"

"Yes, but it's better than if she had no desire to ever get married. Stop being such a glass is half empty kind of guy."

Nick shook his head. "You've lost your mind. I can't even argue with you."

"Listen. We didn't come all this way for nothing. Let's go," Rick said, as he started towards the guard. "My man!" he said as he grabbed the guy's hand and shoulder bumped him as if they were long lost friends.

"What can I do for you?" the guard asked.

"Well, my man here grew up with Melanie Price back when she was Melanie Petrovsky. Anyway, we're in town on business and we thought we'd stop by to see her."

"You should have called her first."

"Well, it's been a while and she changes her number quite a bit. We haven't quite caught up with her."

"I'm sure."

"Seriously. He grew up with her. If you ask her, I'm sure she would love to see him. In fact, take his license with you as proof," Rick said, turning to Nick. "Give him your license."

"I don't want his license. I'm afraid I can't help you."

"Can't help us or won't help us?"

"Can't help you. She's not here."

"What do you mean she's not here? She's in this movie isn't she?"

"Yes. But she's not here. It's a dual set movie and she's on the other set.," the guard answered.

"Where's the other set?" Rick asked.

"Portland."

"Maine?"

"Oregon," the man answered.

"Some source you have," Nick grumbled. "They didn't even bother to tell you she wasn't here?"

"It was a client who's friends with her agent. Went to law school together."

"Must not have been very good friends."

"She *was* here," the guard said. "She left last night."

"When will she be back?"

"She's not coming back as far as I know."

"And how long is she going to be out there?"

"A couple of months."

"We're not going to Oregon," Nick stated as they walked back toward the L.

"You have somewhere else to be?"

"It's a three day drive out there and a week drive back home. Besides, what would be the point?"

"Listen. We're in Chicago and we're five minutes from Wrigley Field, where the Cubs are playing in about two hours. Tell you what. Why don't we take in a game and we can talk about it there?"

"What you mean is, why don't we take in a game so you can try and talk me into more of this ridiculousness."

"Am I that transparent?" Rick asked with a smile.

"As glass," Nick answered before relenting. "Want me to check the box office for tickets? We could sit in the bleachers and catch a home run ball."

"I don't want to sit in the bleachers. I want to throw out the first pitch."

"Yeah, I'm not sure that's going to be possible."

"Anything is possible. Trust me."

~

Rick turned into the VIP parking lot just outside the stadium and gave his name to the attendant. The man was in his 70's, the way all parking attendants seemed to be; most likely retired, working the job to have some interaction with people and maybe catch a few innings of the ballgame.

"Rick McDermott. I should be on the list."

The man tips his glasses up and scans the list, stopping when he finds the name. "Park to the right. Any spot in the 3rd row."

"Thank you, sir."

"Enjoy the game."

"One of your clients give you the tickets?" Nick asked.

"Not a client," Rick answered cryptically.

They entered the stadium through the Player's Entrance and Rick gave the man inside his name.

"Welcome, Mr. McDermott. Turn right and

follow that tunnel all the way to the light at the end of it. Joe said he would meet you there."

"Who's Joe?" Nick asked.

"Joe Mamma. Just relax and enjoy yourself."

Wrigley Field was built in 1914 and had somehow maintained its character, even in the face of adding a few modern amenities such as lights. The interior remained largely untouched. Sparkling clean, but still old cement-filled tunnels and hallways. They followed one such tunnel toward the glistening light at the end of it. A larger than life figure stood at the door, but the sunlight made it impossible to make out much more than a shape. As they drew closer, Nick recognized the Cubs well-chiseled right fielder, Joe Banks.

"As I live and breath—Rick McDermott," Joe said with a smile. "What brings you to this neck of the woods?"

"It's a long story," Rick answered. "Joe, I want you to meet a friend of mine, Nick Nelson. Nick is a bit of a baller himself."

"Well, we're going to find that out," Joe said, as he tossed them both Cubs practice jerseys and caps. "Nice to meet you, Nick."

"You're friends with Joe Banks," Nick announced to no one in particular.

"You seem surprised," Rick grinned.

"I'm just surprised you have a friend," Nick cracked.

"We played ball together at Notre Dame," Joe laughed and they soon found themselves standing on the hallowed infield grass of Wrigley Field.

Joe stepped into the batting cage looking

like a Greek god. His purposeful, powerful swing, sending ball after ball rocketing toward the ivy covered outfield wall. He was enjoying his best season in a career filled with great ones, and had just come off a second place finish in the Home Run Derby All Star weekend. He followed that performance by smashing a home run in the game itself.

"Let's see what you got, McDermott. Grab a bat," Joe said, pointing to the dozen or so bats that leaned up against the cage.

Rick didn't hesitate. He picked up a long, light oak colored bat and swung it once or twice before stepping into the cage. He sent the first pitch he faced into the left field corner.

"Didn't get all of that one," Rick said with a shake of his head.

He sent the second pitch into the Wrigley bleachers. "Didn't get all of that one either," Rick smirked.

"He always was a cocky bastard," Joe laughed to Nick.

"Tell me something I don't know," Nick responded.

A few more solid blasts deep into the Chicago night and Rick finally sent one off the famed old scoreboard behind center field. Players from the Reds had even stepped out of the visitor's dugout to watch.

Rick did the Sammy Sosa clap and flipped the bat end over end. "That one, I got all of," he said with a smile and a wink.

"I don't know why you never went pro after college," Joe said with a shake of his head.

"I decided to go for the big money instead," Rick answered.

"You're up, Nick," Joe urged as Rick cleared the way for him.

Nick was more than a little nervous. Hitting a slo-pitch softball in a Sunday morning beer league was one thing. Taking batting practice in Wrigley Field before the Chicago Cubs, the Cincinnati Reds and the 25,000 or so people that had already filed into the stadium was another.

When he fouled the first pitch off the top of the cage, Joe cracked, "I thought you said this guy was a baller."

But when he laced the second pitch down the left field line, followed by the third pitch down the right field line, Joe nodded his approval. Nick sprayed balls all around Wrigley with such ease that the average fan wouldn't have known he wasn't a member of the Cubs, had he not been wearing flip flops and shorts with his batting practice jersey and cap. On his final swing he caught it just right. Extended his arms. Transferred his weight at the perfect time. Followed through. Back, back, back the ball sailed, eventually finding a home in the bleachers. Nick turned to Rick and Joe with the broadest of grins as several of the Cubs gave him a solid golf clap.

They watched infield practice from the Cubs dugout, chewing and spitting out tobacco like true major leaguers.

"Skip doesn't allow anyone to watch the game from the dugout, not even kids, but I've got you guys seats right next to the dugout," Joe said pointing to a couple of empty seats about ten feet away.

"Joe, I can't thank you enough," Nick said.

"It's the least I could do for my old teammate. He saved my ass in college. We were in the College World Series and I had gone 3 for 3 with a home run and like four RBI's, but we were losing by a run in the bottom of the last inning. I came up with guys on first and second with one out. I struck out, and that's all anyone would have remembered if Rick hadn't laced a two out double to win the game. He bailed me out."

"That's the beauty of sports. I was 0 for 3 before that and I became the hero," Rick responded in a rare show of humility.

"Should we head to our seats?" Nick asked.

"In a minute," Rick said. "Something I have to do first."

"They're ready for you, Mr. McDermott," a pretty girl in a Cubs polo wearing a headset told him.

The announcer began, "Ladies and gentlemen. For tonight's ceremonial first pitch, we'd like to welcome to the mound a long-time Cubs fan and former college teammate of Cubs right fielder, Joe Banks. He had the game winning hit in the 1999 College World Series, lifting Notre Dame to its only title in program history. Please welcome, Rick McDermott!"

Rick patted Nick on the thigh twice playfully before jogging out onto the field.

"Un-fucking-believable," Nick said.

Rick went to the actual pitcher's mound, nodded to the catcher, wheeled, and fired a mid-80's fastball straight down the middle for a strike as the crowd roared.

~

"Ya know, this might be the greatest night of

my life," Nick announced as he tossed a peanut into the air and caught it in his mouth while they watched the game.

"Well, I certainly hope not," Rick laughed. "For a guy whose lifelong goal is to get married, I'm sure your best day is in front of you."

"Well, it sure doesn't seem like that is going to happen anytime soon."

"Maybe it will if we head to Oregon," Rick said with a devilish smile.

"I'm not going to Oregon."

"Why not?"

"I thought we went over this already. It's a three day drive out there for starters. Followed by a week-long drive back. Not to mention she probably won't even remember me. And that's of course if we choose to overlook the fact that she's engaged."

"She probably won't even still be with the guy by the time we get there. You know how those Hollywood types are."

"Do I really want to be with a girl like that?"

"Would you two stop arguing like a couple of teenage girls?" Joe Banks said from the on deck circle directly in front of them on the field. "Check out the black and tan combo sitting eight rows behind the dugout."

All three were now looking at a beautiful brunette and her tan, blonde friend. Both wore flowery, short, summer dresses. The brunette wore glasses, which gave her the appearance of being brighter than she probably was.

"A *C note* says I can get them to meet us at the *Cubby Hole* after the game," Joe said.

"You're on," Rick said.

Joe dropped the donut on his bat by

pounding the bat off the ground. "Excuse me, but I have to go win this thing."

"Another hundred says you strike out," Rick laughed. "And this time, I won't be there to bail you out."

"Deal."

Joe fouled the first pitch off the roof above the press box and stepped out of the batter's box. With a deferential nod to his boys in the stands, he stepped back in and crushed the next pitch over the bleachers and out of the stadium.

"Looks like you're down 200 bucks," Nick remarked as Joe ran by them rubbing his fingers together in the gesture of money.

"We split," Rick said casually. "Those two girls are together."

"Well, obviously."

"No, I mean *together*. I overheard them as I was walking by the line for the ladies room. They're dating."

~

"So this guy claims today was his best day," Rick announced to Joe about Nick as the three of them shared a pitcher after the game.

"It's like that book," Nick said. "*Five Days.* Where the guy dies saving the little boy and is given the opportunity to go back and re-live any five days of his life."

"I know the book," Joe said. "But your *best* day? C'mon."

"Seriously. My life isn't that exciting."

"It really isn't," Rick nodded in agreement. "He hasn't set the bar that high to be fair. All he wants out of life is to find a wife and start a family."

"Well, if you didn't want a family, there would be no reason to find a wife," Joe said.

"That's what I've been trying to tell him."

"Seriously. Joe, you don't have a significant other?" Nick asked hopefully.

"I have a lot of significant others. One in nearly every city we play in."

"You don't want to get married?"

"I'm young and rich. Why the hell would I want to do that?"

"Because you won't always be young."

"But I'll always be rich," Joe laughs as he and Rick bump fists, "and that can buy me a lot of youth."

"You want to know the saddest thing?" Rick asked.

"What's that?"

"He's got a chance to go chase down the one that got away, but he won't do it."

"Why not?"

"You're leaving out some important details. Like the fact that I haven't seen her in 20 years. She's engaged. Oh and she just happens to be one of the most popular movie stars on the planet," Nick answered defensively.

"Who are we talking about?" Joe asked.

"Melanie Price," Rick said.

"No shit?"

"No shit."

"What have you got to lose?" Joe stated.

"You mean besides my dignity?"

"Like he said, what do you have to lose?" Rick smirked.

"We don't even know if we can get on set to talk to her."

"Leave that to me," Rick assured him.

"You would go chasing down this pipe dream?" Nick asked Joe.

"If I was you, yes."

"What's that supposed to mean?!"

"You just said your life isn't that exciting. Make it exciting. Who cares if it works? If you knew it would work out, then it wouldn't be very exciting, now would it?"

"Tell you what," Rick offered, "Let's fly out to Oregon and back into Chicago. Then we can get my car and drive home. I'll pay for the flights."

"You should save your money," Joe said as he nodded toward the door. "Looks like you owe me 200 bucks, pal."

Rick looked up and saw the brunette and blonde from the game approaching them. He reached into his wallet and removed two crisp 100 dollar bills, shaking his head as he slapped them down onto the table.

XII   RIVERBOAT GAMBLERS

*T*wo episodes of *CSI: Miami* and two syndicated *Friends* re-runs helped pass the time on the three and a half hour flight to Portland. They checked in at the River Place Hotel, a shishy, boutique hotel right on the Willamette River in Downtown, and two blocks from the riverboat the movie was filming on.

"My client told me they're filming on the Portland Spirit," Rick said as he rubbed a little gel in his hair.

"Is this the same guy who told us Melanie would be in Chicago yesterday?" Nick chided.

"Yes, but he confirmed it with her agent last night after I bitched him out."

"Wasn't her agent curious as to why he wanted to know?"

"Are you kidding? They get thousands of requests every day. It's good publicity. Plus they have plenty of security. Getting on this boat will be like trying to get into a fortress."

"Then how exactly do you propose we do that?"

"Leave that to me."

"Yes, it's worked out wonderfully so far."

"You took batting practice at Wrigley Field. You chewed gum in the Cubs dugout. You met Joe Banks and the rest of the team. How is that not wonderful?"

"All fair points. Lead the way."

The crowd of people surrounding the pier could be seen the moment they stepped outside the hotel lobby.

"What are all these people doing here?" Nick asked, his optimism now fading.

"Trying to get a glimpse of their favorite movie stars, and maybe an autograph," Rick answered matter-of-factly.

"How are we going to get close enough to even see her much less speak to her? We'll be 25 people back when they wisk her into a car and out of here."

"They're not going to wisk her out here."

"Where then?"

Rick glanced about 200 feet up river to an empty dock save for a lone fisherman. "There," he pointed.

"What do you mean?"

"The white tent that looks like an extension of the boat is probably a pathway for a paddle boat to take someone from the ship to underneath that faraway dock, where they would take those stairs up to a waiting car."

"Lucky fisherman if that's true," Nick said.

"He's not a fisherman. He's security."

"How do you know?"

"For starters, he doesn't have a tackle box. And he doesn't even know how to cast the line. He almost caught it on the back of his shirt a minute ago. And I'd be willing to bet, he's wearing an earpiece. Wanna find out?"

Rick held out a small metal box. It is slightly larger than a smart phone, with a dial on the top.

"What's that?"

"It's a jammer. It's used to jam local radio frequencies with a high pitch sound. Some governments use them when they go to assassinate someone. It blocks all communication."

"Who are you??"

"A client of mine used to work for the CIA."

"Is that thing even legal?"

"Umm, sort of."

"I don't even want to know."

"Let's test it out," Rick said as he gave the dial a quick turn.

The two security men at the main entrance to the ship clutched their heads in agony. The fisherman nearly dropped his pole in the water as he jumped to his feet.

"And there is your answer. C'mon," Rick said, motioning for Nick to follow him.

They walked onto the pier up river from the hysterical screaming of fans trying to get a glimpse of their favorite stars. The fisherman didn't turn around, but they could tell he heard them approach by the fact that he didn't flinch when Rick spoke to him.

"My *mannnn*," Rick began.

Nick rolled his eyes at what he thought was about to be a bad re-run of a show he had already seen.

"What can I do for you?" the fisherman asked, barely turning around.

"Well, my boy here grew up with Melanie Price. They're old friends. Anyway, we're in town for a pharmaceutical convention and we heard she's filming a movie here, so we thought we'd stop by to see if we could visit with her for a few minutes to say hello."

"And you're telling me this, why?" the fisherman said as he stood.

"C'mon, man, I know you're security. Kind of hard to fish if your line doesn't even touch the water," Rick said.

The man looked over the edge of the pier at his rod and reel. The line was in fact, hanging about two feet out of the water.

"Even if I was, what exactly do you expect me to do from here?"

"You know it's my mistake. I forgot to tell you his name. This is Mr. Franklin," Rick said as he thrust a $100 bill into the man's palm.

"Mr. Franklin isn't on the guest list," the man answered.

"Maybe not, but I bet his nine children are," Rick said as he thrust nine more bills into the man's hand.

"I'm afraid they're not on it either. And I can't take your money."

"Sure you can. And while you're putting it in your wallet, just turn your head for a couple of minutes."

The man handed the wad of bills back to him.

"I'm afraid I can't do that."

"Oh, an ethical man," Rick nodded.

"To be honest, you don't have enough money to make it worth my while. Even if Mr. Franklin brought all of his grandchildren and cousins with him."

"I wouldn't be so sure of that," Rick smiled. "What do they pay you guys? A couple hundred bucks a day?"

"Let's just say they pay us well enough so that we don't need to take tips. And your thousand bucks won't pay my mortgage when I get fired."

"Fair enough," Rick agreed. "How about I appeal to your sympathetic side instead? This guy hasn't gotten laid in so long that Darwin would be worried for him."

"I think you mean, Lamark," the man answered. "Darwin referred to Survival of the Fittest. Lamark believed something that wasn't used would eventually disappear."

"An educated man as well," Rick nodded. "I'm impressed."

"I'm standing right here, you know," a frustrated Nick interjected. He had been silent until that point.

"Listen," Rick said. "My boy here is the last of the nice guys. You would want him to date your sister."

The guard laughed.

"All he wants is to spend ten minutes catching up with an old friend. That's it. I bet if you told her he was out here, she would tell you to let him in."

"I wish I could help you. I really do. But I can't let you in through here. And we're not allowed to contact the actors."

Rick nodded. "I hear ya. Well, thanks anyway."

"What I can do," the guard added as they began to walk away, "is send you to the main entrance of the ship."

"There's like a thousand people out there."

"There won't be a thousand people on the list of 75 extras who get to go on the boat," the man said.

"My *MANNNNN!*" Rick said as he shook hands with the hulking man and pulled him in for a shoulder bump.

"I can't promise you'll get to talk to her, or even see her for that matter. But you'll be on the boat."

"We really appreciate it," Nick said.

"Better tell me what your real names are so I can call over there. They'll want to see your license, *Mr. Franklin.*"

"Rick McDermott. And Nick Nelson. And thanks again."

~

"I have no idea how you managed to pull that off," Nick said with a shake of his head.

"I'm a very likeable guy," was Rick's response, which both of them knew wasn't true until he added, "when I want to be."

They showed their licenses at the entrance after walking by a thousand envious people who wondered who they were, and if they were famous.

"You guys are going to go to the dining room," the casting director said.

"Do we need to change clothes or anything?" Rick asked, pointing to the wardrobe room.

"No. What you're wearing is perfect."

"What's this movie about?"

"About a lonely guy who falls in love with a wannabe actress who makes her living singing on a riverboat. He rides the boat four times a week every week, until one day she strikes up a conversation with him."

"What's it called?"

"The Last of the Nice Guys."

Rick slowly turned to Nick as if to silently remind him it was fate.

XIII THE VOICE OF AN ANGEL

*S*eventeen year old, Nick Nelson, clad in his high school letterman's jacket, stepped off the curb and was nearly mowed down by a *Fiat* that raced past. Nick looked as out of place in Rome as a deer in New York City. He sprinted across the street and boarded a waiting tour bus with a few friends and settled into a seat about halfway back.

Melanie Price, then Melanie Petrovsky, also seventeen, was the last one to board. Her overweight and impatient teacher checked his watch, and said admonishingly, "Miss Petrovsky. Next time we won't wait for you. And if your tardiness continues, we'll put you back on a plane for the states.

"I'm so sorry," she said quietly, "I couldn't find my..."

But he didn't want to hear it. Simply waved her away. She responded by sticking her tongue out at him once he had turned his back. Melanie smiled once she realized Nick had been watching her admiringly. She grabbed a seat across the aisle from him.

"He can be a real jerk sometimes."

"Sometimes?" Nick smiled.

"Well, most of the time."

"You should have told him you were having

female problems. Men never know how to respond to that.

"Oh, god. I could never. I'd be too embarrassed."

Nick offered his hand in friendship. "I'm Nick Nelson."

"Please?" Melanie responded at barely above a whisper. It took him a moment to realize that this was her ever-so-polite and adorable way of saying she hadn't heard him correctly.

"Nick...Nelson."

"Well, which is it?" she laughed. "Nick? Or Nelson?"

"It's both," he answered, puzzled.

"I know. I'm just teasing. I'm Melanie Petrovsky. I hate my name, by the way. I'm going to change it once I become a famous actress."

"To what?" Nick asked.

"Something short. One syllable. Non-denominational."

"How about Price?"

"Melanie Price. I like it."

"Where are you from, Melanie Price?"

"Cincinnati. You?"

"I'm from the C – T," Nick said, trying to be cool.

"New York City?"

"Not the *city*. The Sea – Tee. Connecticut."

Melanie laughed when she finally realized what he was saying. "Ohhh. The C – T."

And from that moment on, from the crumbling steps inside the Roman Coliseum, to a gondola ride in Venice, to a cave just off the island of Capri, to the mist covered streets of

Florence; they were inseparable.

Their hotel in Florence was a historic landmark. Wood floors. Paint peeling from the walls. Hand-held showerheads in the bathrooms. It was a place whose charm he would have appreciated much more 20 years later, but as a seventeen year old, it was simply old and inconvenient. Who wants to hold a showerhead while you try to shampoo your hair?

Nick knocked softly on a door in the dimly lit hallway. Melanie opened it a few seconds later.

"It's your last night in Florence. You should have gone with your friends. Who knows when you'll ever be here again?"

"Nonsense. Besides, I couldn't very well leave you all alone in the creeper hotel."

"I'd have been fine," she smiled, "but thank you."

"It wasn't you I was worried about," Nick winked. "I can't believe that jerk placed you on 'hotel room arrest' for saying 'God Bless You' and offering someone a tissue while he was talking."

Melanie grabbed a sweater that was hanging over a chair. "Well, since it's probably only a matter of time before I get in trouble again, I might as well at least deserve it. Let's go get something to eat."

The elevator doors opened. Eight people were already inside an elevator built for six. They slid over to make room for two more. Nick hesitated; it wasn't his nature even then to take an unnecessary chance, but Melanie pulled him inside by taking his hand. The metal, grated doors closed and the creaking elevator began its descent. About three floors down, an eerie *snapping* of a cable preceded a rapid free-fall. A young couple began shouting in Italian. *Everyone* clutched the walls of the elevator in desperation. Seconds later, an emergency cable caught, and the hurtling box jolted to an abrupt halt, sending everyone tumbling to the floor in a heap.

"You ok?" Nick asked.

"I'm fine," she answered unfazed. "You?"

"I'm ok. But I am a bit claustrophobic."

She didn't *say* anything. She simply rested her head gently on his shoulder. He seemed surprised at first; then leaned his on top of hers. Two hours later, the rusty doors of the elevator were finally pried open half a floor above them. One by one, each person was lifted out, with Nick remaining as the last one.

"Let it not be said that I don't know how to show a girl a good time," Nick said as he climbed out.

Two days later they returned to Rome for their final night in Europe, each group going out on their own. Nick returned to the hotel first and fell asleep in a chair on the terrace after downing a bottle of wine. He had drank alcohol plenty of times back home, but it was usually on the sly or in the back parking lot of his school. It was a strange feeling being able to drink out in the open in Europe at seventeen. It kind of took the fun out of it. Not that it stopped them. Several other students were passed out in various parts of the room.

Melanie pushed open the door that had been propped open by the latch and peered in. She smiled when she eyed Nick asleep in the chair on the balcony and woke him with a soft kiss on the cheek. He looked up with a start of someone who thought they were being attacked.

"I'm so sorry I woke you," she smiled, "but you just looked so incredibly cute sitting there I couldn't resist.

Nick attempted to rub the sleep from his eyes. "Yeah, my mother always says I'm at my best when I'm sleeping. Not sure exactly what that means, but..." he said, his voice trailing off to her laughter.

"Thanks for waiting up for me," she said sarcastically.

"I actually was trying to. I just wasn't doing a very good job of it."

"I can't believe we're all leaving tomorrow. I'm going to miss you. Who's going to keep me out of trouble?" she lamented.

"I'm not sure that's possible, but it's a job I would readily accept in a nanosecond," Nick answered.

"A nanosecond? That sounds pretty quick."

"It's the quickest there is."

The two of them managed to stake out a quarter of a queen sized bed in the other room, sharing it with three other people, lying across it. Nick awakened as the first rays of sunshine forced their way into the room and stretched carelessly, sending an elbow directly into Melanie's forehead before actually opening his eyes.

"Oh, my god," he exclaimed when he realized what he had done. "I'm so sorry, Mel."

"It's ok," she smiled her soft smile. "The bruise will go nicely with the bruise on my back

I got from rolling onto the floor in the middle of the night."

Nick glanced around the room. In addition to the people on the bed, approximately a half dozen other people were littered across the floor. "Not the most romantic setting," he said.

"Now that you mention it...but until just now, I hadn't really noticed."

Nick searched for what he wanted to say. "You know, I'm not very good at goodbyes. So, if you don't see me at the bus when you leave, don't take it personally."

"I'll try not to."

"It's just that every time I say goodbye to someone I care about, it seems like I never end up seeing them again. I said goodbye to my grandmother two summers ago before I went away to camp, and she died while I was away. I said goodbye to my best friend from high school this past Christmas, and I never saw him again either. He died in a car accident..." he continued, his voice trailing off.

"I understand. But I promise you'll see me again—if you want to."

"Of course I want to."

"Then you will."

~

"You're joking, right?" Rick said once Nick was finished relaying the story to him.

"What?"

"What?!! Is there no limit to your patheticness? At least tell me you got her drunk and had your way with her."

"But that wouldn't be true. And she would know."

"The hell with her. Good god, man, at least

give me some glimmer of hope that I haven't dragged myself clear across the country for a completely lost cause."

"She isn't like that. She's sweet."

"Maybe she was then, but I guarantee you she isn't now. She's beautiful, talented, rich and famous. She probably has 10 people on payroll whose sole job is to blow sunshine up her ass. There isn't a person on the planet who wouldn't be an ahole in her shoes."

"Then why would I want to be with someone like that?"

"It doesn't make her a bad person. It just means you've got to be a little more interesting. Hell, I'm only three of those things and I'm an ahole. But I'm likeable as hell."

"That's debatable."

"Can you imagine if someone put me on the cover of GQ? I'd probably be insufferable."

"One could make the argument that you already are."

"Look, pal, I'm just trying to help you here. And your elevator story that she probably doesn't even remember, about her leaning her head on your shoulder isn't going to cut it. You've got one shot at this, and if you fail, it's back to your endless abyss of misery for the rest of your miserable life."

"Thanks for the pep talk."

"No problem."

"Ladies and gentlemen, we really appreciate you being a part of our film in today's scenes on the Portland Spirit!" a short, poorly dressed, bearded man in a baseball cap shouted out with manufactured excitement. "In a few minutes, we will begin filming our main scenes, but for now we'd like you to enjoy the riverboat jazzland stylings of the Philip Hall Orchestra while we film our cutaway shots. Just carry on with your normal conversations as we'll be dubbing them out in editing. Best way to help us is for you to just be yourselves. Thanks again for being a part of this."

Entering the room at that moment unannounced was Melanie's leading man, James Fullman. He sat by himself at the empty table next to Rick and Nick. They hadn't even noticed it was empty until that moment.

"He looks older than dirt," Rick whispered, nowhere near as quietly as he thought he had.

"Shhhhh!" Nick admonished.

"It's true."

"First of all, he's #10 on People's Sexiest Men Alive list. And secondly, the heavy makeup ruins actors complexions after a while."

"First of all, if he's #10, I should be numbers 1 and 2. You could be 3. And secondly, why do they wear so much makeup then?"

"They need it for the lighting. It cuts down on the glare and hides blemishes. Makes them look younger than they are."

"Maybe on film, but in person it just makes them look old. You can old or you can look weird, but you can't look young again."

The band began by playing *When the Saints Come Marching In*. Several people tapped their hands and feet to the music. When they followed up with Glenn Miller's *In the Mood*, people began snapping their fingers. Rick swayed his shoulders and moved his arms back and forth in rhythm.

Be yourselves the director had said. Big mistake where Rick McDermott was concerned. He was soon on his feet and sauntering over to a table of ladies. He had one of them on the dance floor before Nick could even react.

Spinning her. Pushing her away. Pulling her close for a dip. Lifting this complete stranger over his head, then sliding her between his legs. Nick panicked that they would be asked to leave before he even got to lay eyes on Melanie. But the rest of the room had soon joined Rick on the dance floor. It looked like American Bandstand.

James Fullman went right along with it and approached the two remaining ladies that were not already dancing. He nodded for Nick to join him to dance with the other one. He did so, somewhat awkwardly, even more so when he realized the camera was directly on them. But he made the most of it, moving his 75 year old partner across the floor with the subtlety of a tractor trailer in an antique shop. But everyone was enjoying themselves, so he allowed himself to.

The song ended to a rousing ovation from the audience. It was such a spontaneous display that the director signaled to keep rolling film. It was pure gold as they said in Hollywood.

And then out of nowhere, a voice, so soft, so peaceful and serene. Borderline haunting in a good way. No, an incredible way. As Melanie Price made her way on stage singing *Every*

Time We Say Goodbye, she so mesmerized the audience that they all found their way to their seats, just so they could fully appreciate what they were hearing. Even Rick sat without a word. While one camera was focused on Melanie, the other was on Nick, who wore the exact expression the director wanted his lead actor to wear—one of a person who was completely oblivious that anyone other than Melanie was even in the room. And for Nick Nelson, no one else was.

XIV   REUNITED AT LONG LAST

"*W*ell, we found finally found where they were filming, you talked our way on to the set, and we even managed to see her," Nick said once they had taken a break from filming. "The question now is how do we get her to notice me?"

"She noticed you," Rick assured him.

"What makes you say that?"

"Because she froze at the beginning of the song during the 1st of her 17 takes."

"Maybe she forgot the words?"

"It wasn't that kind of freeze."

"Oh please do tell me what kind of freeze it was."

"It was the kind of freeze that happens when you see someone you didn't expect to see. Either that, or she shit her pants."

"She did not shit her pants!" Nick laughed.

"Well then she noticed you," Rick stated again.

"She hasn't seen me in 20 years. I doubt she'd even recognize me."

"Are you kidding me? You probably look the same as you did in 8th grade."

"I do not look the same as I did in 8th grade," Nick protested.

"Sure you do.   You probably looked like you

were 40 when you were eight, and you'll look like you're 40 when you're 80. You're just one of those guys. You aged early and haven't aged since."

"Thanks. I think. I still think you're crazy."

"Then put your money where your mouth is," Rick said as he removed a crisp one hundred dollar bill from his money clip.

"100 bucks?" Nick asked.

"Let's go big guy. Get your money on the table."

Nick figured it was a no lose situation. He would either pick up a quick 100 bucks, or he would get to speak to his long lost love. He slapped the C note on the table. Rick picked them both up.

"What are you doing?" Nick asked just before he heard the sweet female voice behind him.

"Excuse me," she said softly.

Nick spun around so quickly his head nearly flew off his shoulders.

"I'm sorry to bother you," she continued quietly. "But you look exactly like someone I used to know."

"Nick Nelson?" Rick offered.

She broke into a wide smile. "Nick? Is that really you?"

Rick kicked him under the table square in the shin in an effort to get him to stand up.

"Hi Mel," he said as he slowly stood up, rubbing his leg.

"What are you doing here?" she asked excitedly.

"We're in town for a couple of meetings and I heard you were filming here, so we tried to bribe security to get in and when that didn't work, we signed up to be extras."

"You should have asked them to come get me."

"We tried that, but they weren't going for it. They were very forbidding."

She laughed a familiar laugh. Soft and sweet and for the briefest of moments, he was taken back in time. But he quickly felt dozens of eyes upon them, wondering who exactly he was. She pulled him away from the crowd.

"Where are you staying?"

"At the RiverPlace."

"So am I," she answered. "Would you like to meet up for breakfast tomorrow or something?"

"I'd...love to," he managed to stammer.

She hugged him unexpectedly tightly. He was stiff as a board until the warmth of her hug caused him to eventually wrap his arms around her in return. Melanie kissed him softly on the lips, before she disappeared behind the curtains to be fussed over by a dozen wardrobe people. Nick instinctively touched the lips she just kissed as he fell back into his chair.

"What do you have to say now?" Rick asked.

"Nothing. Nothing at all."

"That's what I thought."

~

Every set of eyes inside the restaurant as well as a couple of dozen eyes peering in from outside the window were firmly focused on the man who was having breakfast with the most popular movie star in the world and Nick Nelson didn't like it at all. After spending his entire childhood and the majority of his adult life blending into rooms like taupe wallpaper, he was unaccustomed to being the center of attention. It unnerved him so much so that he must have hand combed his hair and checked his nose for the stray booger bullet at least a dozen times before Melanie tried to calm him down.

"You look really nice. And your hair is perfect," she smiled.

"Doesn't this bother you?"

"Please?"

Her response froze Nick for an instant. It took him back to a much simpler time.

"This—the constant attention and lack of privacy."

"Ohhhh. It used to, but I don't notice it much anymore. After a couple of terrible photographs in magazines and on the entertainment shows, I stopped going out of the house unless my hair and makeup were perfect!" she laughed. "Eventually, that got old, so I had a choice to make. Don't go out looking anything less than perfect, or don't read magazines, watch TV or surf the internet."

"That doesn't sound like much of a life."

"Life is one big trade off," Melanie said as she made her way through a Cobb Salad.

"So how does a Midwestern girl like living in Los Angeles?"

"Surprisingly, I like it a lot. There's just something amazing about waking up every day to sunshine. There's always something to do. You almost never have to cancel or change your plans..."

"Don't you miss the change of seasons?" Nick asked.

"I still get to experience them when I visit

my family."

"How is your family?"

"They're good. Parents are getting older, which is sad and more noticeable when you don't see them all the time. How's your family?"

"They're all gone unfortunately. Except for my sister and brother-in-law. On holidays, we used to have two full tables of people. Now there's just three of us. It's not bad. It's nice actually, being closer to my sister than when we were younger. Just different."

"I'm really sorry," Melanie answered. "Your parents were so sweet, and funny and smart."

"They always liked you."

"It's funny you say that, because the last time I was home, my mother and I were looking through some old pictures and came upon one from high school of you and I in Florence. My mother asked whatever happened to you. She said, 'I always thought the two of you would end up together.'"

An uncomfortable silence followed.

"Then you had to go off and become this big movie star," Nick said in an effort to break the awkwardness. "So is it everything you hoped it would be? I realize that's probably a dumb question."

"I like the process of acting. And reading scripts and books searching for the right project. The money's not bad either," she smiled.

"I imagine it's better than not bad," he chuckled.

"For a few years anyway. And then it's off to the plastic surgeon in a futile attempt to prolong my flailing career."

"Don't do that," Nick urged. "You won't need it. You've aged well. More importantly, you're a good actress."

"Well, thank you," she blushed.

"Besides, as a friend of mine says; *you can look old, or you can look weird, but you can't look young again.*"

"That's awful!"

"He claims it's true. He does have a point. Pretty easy to tell when someone has had plastic surgery. It doesn't look natural."

"Well that's depressing. But enough about me. I'd rather hear about you and what's new in *your* life since we last spoke."

"Now *that* is a depressing topic. Nothing exciting I'm afraid."

"In ten years?!"

"Sad, but true. I'm the Executive Producer for a small town talk show in Connecticut."

"That doesn't sound bad at all. How long have you been doing that?"

"About eight years now."

"Well, it must be doing pretty well to still be on the air."

"It's ok."

"But...."

"But a day has rarely gone by in the past five years where I haven't wished it would either get cancelled, or I would get fired."

"I'm not sure I follow you."

"I've met some great people working there, and the pay isn't bad, but I feel like it's time for a change."

"Then why don't you try something different?"

"I'm thinking about it. It's just tough to walk away from a steady pay check."

"I understand what you mean. I've always wanted to do Broadway, but it's tough to sacrifice the pay of the big screen when you don't know how long you'll be on the *it* list."

Nick tried to explain further what he meant, "You know how when you're younger, you plan your entire life out with these lofty dreams. And then as you get older you realize they're just not going to happen. You're not going to be the point guard for the Knicks, or a State Senator, or marry the Queen of Sheeba. So you reassess. And this time, you set goals that you know are attainable. Like finding a steady job in a city where you're comfortable. You settle. Unless of course you're you."

"Is that what you've done? Settle?"

Nick nodded, "In every aspect of my life except for love. That is one area I refuse to compromise."

"That might be the most romantic thing I've everheard," she gushed.

"Yeah, we'll see how romantic it seems when I'm 86 years old and sipping my lunch through a straw by myself in a nursing home."

"I guess we have both settled in opposite ways," she said quietly.

"Now, I'm not sure I'm following *you*."

"Bill's a great guy. He's an amazing actor. He's Hollywood royalty. On paper it works."

"And in the real world?"

"He doesn't make me laugh."

"Well, he's old. Maybe he just needs some new material. Charlie Chaplin routines went out years ago."

"He's not *that* old," she laughed.

"Or maybe he's very funny, and you just don't have a sense of humor. Ever think about that, Smarty-Pants?"

She threw a crumpled napkin at him.

"I'm trying to be serious!"

"Being serious is overrated. But ok ok. If you don't love him, then why are you with him?"

She thought it over for a moment before responding.

"I love him. I'm just not *in love* with him," she whispered quietly and hopefully out of the curious eyes and ears that were straining to hear any part of their conversation.

~

Nick walked into the hotel room just in time to see Rick sink a ten-foot putt into a plastic cup in the middle of the sitting area.

"How'd you hit 'em today?"

"Wonderfully as always. Shot a 76. How was lunch?"

"It was ok."

"Just ok?"

"Maybe slightly better than ok."

"Dental work is less painful than this. What happened?!"

"She's not in love with her fiancée for one thing."

"That's great news!"

"I suppose it is."

"You suppose? When are you going to see her again?"

"Tonight for dinner. And you're coming with."

"Me?! Why would you want me there?"

"Because you're always claiming to be an

excellent read of women. I want to see what you think. Is she interested in me? Or is she just interested in getting out of her current situation? Plus, she really wants to meet the person who said '*you can look old, or you can look weird, but you can't look young again.*'"

"Truer words were never spoken."

XV   A DISH BEST SERVED COLD

*T*hey sat in the bar area of an out of the way restaurant that wouldn't be out of the way much longer once word got out who had visited it. Nick pulled back a chair for Melanie to sit in and introduced Rick.

"Mel, I'd like you to meet a friend of mine. This is Rick McDermott."

"Nice to meet you, Rick," she responded while shaking his hand.

"It's a pleasure. So, I hear you're not in love with your fiancée."

His comment caught Nick taking a sip of water. He spit it onto the tablecloth mid sip.

"What? Was I not supposed to say that?"

"Uh, yeah."

Melanie smiled softly. "It's ok. Bill's a good man."

"So are a lot of people.   But why are you with him?"

"Because it's comfortable I guess."

"So are my boxers, but I'm not planning on marrying them."

She laughed, which eased the tension a bit in Nick's mind at least. "I guess I got tired of watching all my friends get married and began to worry that before too long I'd have a better chance of getting struck by lightning than getting married."

"I like your way of thinking and I agree with it. Hell, I can't think of five women over the age of 40 that I'd want to sleep with. But you look young. You've still got a couple of good years left in you."

"Gee, thanks."

"So go land yourself someone you're attracted to. Before it's too late."

Why had he invited him to dinner again? At that moment, Nick couldn't think of a single reason.

"There's more to a relationship than physical attraction," Nick chimed in.

"Don't be ridiculous," Rick said with a dismissive wave.

"Aren't you the same man who once told me, and I quote, 'For every hot chick, there's some dude who's tired of banging her?' Obviously, when that happens, you need to have a friendship to fall back on."

"You misunderstood me."

"Did you, or did you not say that?"

"Yes, I said it, but what I meant was that I don't think it's possible for a man and a woman to stay together forever."

"Why not? You have friendships that last a lifetime. Why not a husband and wife?"

"Simple. Because you're allowed to have more than one friend."

Nick nodded and laughed. It was tough to argue with him. "The world according to Rick McDermott."

"I can't help that I'm a truth teller," Rick said as he turned to Melanie. "Now, Mel. I don't know you very well. In fact, I don't know you at all. But I know women. And I know there is no way a woman like you should be with a pretentious, opinionated, old man actor who drives a Prius when he can afford any 20 cars he wants."

"How do you know Bill drives a Prius?"

"Because all pretentious, liberal actor-types drive Priuses to make themselves feel better about being ridiculously overpaid."

"Oh my God," Nick moaned.

"Don't get me wrong. I don't begrudge anyone for making money. Just don't try to pretend you don't have it."

"Maybe he's just socially aware," Nick offered.

"Maybe. Maybe he's a great guy. But you still don't need a guy like that. You need a guy who's going to rip your clothes off the second you walk through the door. And he won't care if the blinds are up, if the neighbors can see in, or the kids are upstairs. He'll take you right there on the kitchen floor, because he can't even wait to get you onto the living room couch."

"Oh...my...God...Mel, I'm so sorry."

"You might be right," she answered as Nick's head spun towards her as if on a swivel. He definitely hadn't expected that response.

"I know I'm right. You were a theatre major in college, weren't you? I thought I read that somewhere."

"Yes. Then what are you doing making superhero movies? You should go to New York and work on Broadway, where anything worth while in this country happens."

"The pay isn't quite the same," she said.

"Give me a break. Your last reported movie quote was 18 mill a film and you made four movies last year alone. You couldn't spend your money in ten lifetimes."

"I always have wanted to live in New York. But Bill hates it there."

Rick's attention suddenly turned to the television a few feet away from them at the bar.

"What is it?"

They all turned to the commercial on the TV. A man was speaking. *"I'm Jim Cook, President of Samuel Adams, voted the best beer in America seven years in a row. And we thought, what better way for you to get a look at why our frost brewed beer is so good, than by showing you how we make it."*

He continued to speak while he walked on a tour of the brewery. *"We begin by making certain the environment we make our beer in is clean and sterile."*

He opened the door and revealed a man, wearing a dirty undershirt, smoking a cigarette, with no gloves on. The man scratched himself in his private area, and looked around for an ashtray. When he couldn't find one, he shrugged and dumped the ashes into one of the bottles that was coming by on the conveyor belt.

"Next is the place we actually make our frost brewed lagers and ales. Our unique brewing process may take a little longer, but in the end, we think it's worth it."

He opened another door, this time revealing five men, each pissing in a bottle. When finished, each placed the bottle back on the belt.

The entire bar was now focused on the

television like it was game seven of the World Series. Most of them looked horrified.

"And finally, each batch of Sam Adams is checked for color, texture, and of course, taste..."

Behind a 3rd door was a half-naked man, surrounded by mostly naked beautiful women, as he took a big swig of a Sam Adams. The man immediately grimaced and spat the beer out.

"This tastes like piss!" he screamed.

The people in the bar roared. One man doubled over from laughter. Another looked like he was about to piss his pants. A 3rd man was actually drinking a Sam Adams. He looked at it skeptically and placed it down on the bar without taking another sip. The bartender replaced it with a Corona.

"Mel, could you excuse us for a minute?" Nick said as he turned to Rick. "Can I speak with you?"

Rick knew the conversation that was about to take place. He followed him to the other side of the bar.

"You're responsible for that aren't you?"

"Define responsible."

"You edited that together in *my* editing bay."

"You may not believe this, but I never intended for it to air over national TV. Protocol is for them to screen it for their client first before putting it on the air live. But Bill is an idiot. Obviously, he didn't do either."

"If you expect me to work with you, you can't keep pulling stuff like this. What if they trace it back to you?"

"They can't don't worry."

Rick's cell phone rang. "Hold that thought," he said as he answered it. "Hello. Peter. How are you? Yes, I just saw it as a matter of fact. It was a rather unusual approach. The people at the bar I'm at seemed to enjoy it if that's any consolation. Well, I'm in Portland right now, but I'll be back Tuesday if you'd like to meet. I'll see you then." He hung up. "Pete Cook. Wants to come with us. You were saying?"

"I was saying that if expect me to join you, you can't keep pulling that sort of thing."

"I promise," Rick said as his eyes shifted back to the television. "But if you didn't appreciate that, you're *really* going to hate this."

During a 60 second news update, the local anchor announced, *"Shocking news out of New York City this evening as 55 year old William Griggs, Co-Founder of the Pressman-Griggs Advertising Agency, was arrested and charged with two counts of sexual assault on a minor and possession of cocaine. That's more bad news for one of the top agencies in the world, who recently lost a number of top clients when four of its executives left to start up their own firm..."*

Nick seemed to be in a state of equal parts shock and disgust.

"He's not a good guy," Rick reasoned.

Nick waved him off and headed back to the table.

"The girl's not even going to press charges," he yelled after him. "She's going to tell them she lied about her age. And there was only enough coke for about 90 days of jail time. He'll probably just get a slap on the wrist. Community service. It'll do him some good!"

Nick arrived back at the table. Rick arrived a few seconds later.

"Everything ok?" Melanie asked.

Nick nodded. "Everything's fine."

"Did you guys see that commercial? It was hilarious. Although I don't know what they were thinking."

Nick glared at Rick. "I don't know what they were thinking either."

"Well, I'm going to turn in," Rick said.

"You sure you can't stay for a little bit?" Melanie asked.

Nick made no such effort to talk him out of it.

"I'm really tired. Plus, you guys have a lot to catch up on. But maybe I'll see you tomorrow. I don't know what your filming schedule is, but Nick are I were going to take in Multnomah Falls."

"We are actually off tomorrow, so that might work."

"It was nice to meet you," Rick said.

"Likewise."

"I'll see you later, buddy," he said to Nick, who barely nodded in acknowledgment. He was pretty peeved.

"Your friend is very entertaining," Melanie said once he had left.

"That is one of many words that could be used to describe him. One of the nicer ones I might add. I'm sorry if he crossed the line a bit."

"Don't be. He was actually pretty accurate

in his assessment of me."

"So what are you going to do then?"

"I'm going to get married, because it's the safe play. And because it's not easy determining whether someone is wrong for you, when on paper at least, they seem right."

"My mother once told me that when you meet the right person, you know it immediately. And by that logic, if you meet someone and don't know that they're right, then they must be wrong."

"I admire you, Nick, for your refusal to settle for anything less than you're looking for. I know my life will turn out all right. But it also won't be the magical one yours will be either."

"I don't know about magical."

"It will be."

"Yours could be the same. You control your own destiny."

She hesitated at coming clean with the cold, hard truth. "I know. But the only thing I fear more than ending up with the wrong person; is ending up with no person at all."

~

Nick lied awake on his bed and looked over at the empty one next to him that hadn't been slept in all night. A key card was suddenly swiped through the scanner on the door, and Rick entered quietly.

"Thought you were tired last night?" Nick said.

"I was. But then I ran into these 24 year old twins in the lobby on my way up."

"Did you sleep with *both* of them?"

"Neither of them," Rick laughed.

"You must be losing your touch."

Rick feigned being offended. "I'm not that kind of guy."

"Not that kind of guy?! You're the *reason* there's the *saying* 'that kind of guy'."

"Not anymore. I'm a changed man. Must be your influence."

"Passed out, huh?"

"Just wasn't feeling it. So anyway I ended up getting into a shot drinking contest with the Seattle Seahawks in the hotel bar instead."

"Which ones?"

"Most of them I think. They're in town for a pre-season mini-camp. Ended up passing out on a couch in one of their rooms. You still pissed at me?" Rick asked.

"Not as much as I probably should be. The commercial was pretty funny." They both shared a laugh.

"So how'd your night end up?"

"We had a few drinks. Laughed a bit. Then hugged and kissed each other good night."

"That's it?"

"That's it."

"Did you at least talk about the two of you?"

"What about the two of us?"

"Getting together."

"We're not going to get together."

"Why not?"

"Because I'm not feeling it."

"But what about that special feeling you had the first time you met her? That special *moment.*" Rick used the forefinger and middle finger on both hands as quotes for emphasis.

"We were 17 then. Before yesterday, we hadn't even seen each other in 20 years. People change."

"I just think it's a shame. You're both good people. You're tired of being alone. And she's looking for a way out of her relationship."

"That's not a reason to get together."

"So what's she going to do? Is she going to go through with the wedding?"

"Two weeks from now, as far as I know. Unless, of course, someone can give her a reason not to."

"I can give her a reason. She's not in love with the guy."

"Well, then that's something you'll have to take up with her I guess," Nick said as he smiled a knowing smile. "She's going to Multnomah Falls with us tomorrow."

XVI   CLIMBING MULTNOMAH

"*I* thought we were climbing a waterfall?" Rick asked. "What are we doing at the public library?"

"Mel is making a public appearance at a literacy program for kids, so we're stopping here first," Nick answered as he held open the door at a side entrance.

"Do you think she'll be wearing glasses with her hair pulled up, a tight skirt, heels and a lowly buttoned blouse?"

"They're not filming a Van Halen video. It's for six year olds."

"Boooorrrring."

Melanie was reading to a group of pre-schoolers in a back room when they entered. Nick grabbed a seat off to the side not far from her, while Rick wandered among the stacks of books.

"*Beauty comes from within, he told her. It's in the eye of the beholder*," Melanie read.

A little boy raised his hand.

"Yes, Matthew?"

"What's a beholder?"

"It's someone who is looking at you."

"Then why don't they say 'Beauty is in the eye of whoever is looking at you?'"

"I guess they think 'beholder' sounds better," she laughed.

"I think it's confusing."

"I think so too," a little girl chimed in.

"You might be right," Melanie smiled.

Standing amongst the dozen or so reporters that were snapping photographs, his eyes peering over the top of a book entitled *Sarcasm as Your Best Friend,* was Rick. Melanie scooped up a crying little boy, and hoisted him onto her lap without missing a beat of the story she was reading. Neither reading nor little kids were normally of interest to Rick, but for some reason, he couldn't take his eyes off of her.

Long after she had finished reading, Melanie stayed to sign every piece of paper thrust in front of her and posed for pictures. What was supposed to be a quick, barely publicized stop had turned into much more, as it always did.

"I just want to stop by the hotel to change before we head out to the falls," she said to them both as they waited patiently. Well, Nick waited patiently, Rick, not so much.

"What's wrong with what you're wearing?" Nick asked.

"I need to put on something a little less conspicuous or we won't have any privacy all day. I know that sounds just horribly conceited and I really don't mean it to, but it's the way my life is these days."

When she stepped into the living room area of her penthouse suite, the expression on Nick's face said he was thinking everything Rick was about to say.

"You're joking, right?" Rick blurted out.

"What?" she responded as she self-consciously looked herself over.

"I thought you said you wanted to be *in*conspicuous?"

"I do."

"Well nothing screams attention like tight leopard print pants, Steve Madden shoes, a low-cut top and over-sized sunglasses. You gotta lose the outfit."

"Nick?" She looked at him for support. He shrugged and winced. "Great. So what am I supposed to wear?"

"Do you have black yoga pants?" Rick asked.

"Of course."

"Put them on with a t-shirt, and lose the sunglasses. I'll bring you a sweatshirt and a baseball cap. And put on some Nike's for God's sake."

When he returned a few minutes later, two hulking men answered the hotel room door.

"What's the deal with Hanz and Franz?" Rick said.

"They're my security. Terry and Steve."

"Yeah, you guys might want to—you know what? You're pretty much going to stand out no matter what you wear so we might as well just get going."

He tossed Melanie a navy Notre Dame hoodie and a Nike running cap that she had to adjust to the smallest setting for it to fit.

"Perfect," Rick told her.

"You don't think they'll recognize me?"

"They'll think you'll look familiar, but by the time they figure it out, we will be long past them."

She looked to Nick once again for his approval.

"You look great," he said, which seemed to put her mind at ease.

The bridge halfway up Multnomah Falls had been a postcard and poster fixture for years, but none of them even came close to doing the setting justice. The Benson Bridge sat about halfway up and in front of the second highest falls in the United States that reached 621 feet at its peak. The smell of the evergreens along the walk path along with the occasional mist from the falls impressed even the normally unimpressible Rick.

After taking the obligatory pictures pretending to throw and kick each other off the bridge, they continued another half mile to the top of the falls. And not one person recognized Melanie.

"Ok, so you love Bill, but you're not *in love* with him," Rick began. "He's Hollywood Royalty who you think has given credibility to your career, but you've made ten times as much money as he has."

"He's won two Academy Awards."

"Would you rather have an Academy Award that will double as a paperweight in your home office, where only the five people that actually saw the movie care about, or be beloved by tens of millions of fans?"

"Can't I have both?"

"No, you can't. Until you're seventy, and making a comeback after ten years away from making movies. Then they'll give you an award because they feel sorry for you that you're looks have faded, and everyone will go to see the aging former beauty queen."

"That's depressing."

"Do you even miss him when he's not around?"

"Of course."

"Not as a friend or a relative. Do you *really* miss him?"

"I guess."

"You guess?!" Rick exclaimed. "That would be a no then. Look, we're not trying to make you feel badly or lecture you on love. Ok, maybe we are. But Nick's an expert. He's the guy who believes in true love. He knows what to look for. And Nick, what are you always telling me about when you'll know if you've met the right person?"

Nick hesitated a moment before answering. He didn't want to come across as piling on. "It's not the person where everything seems perfect that's the one. It's the person that makes no sense for you, where everything seems wrong, but you want to be with them anyway."

Melanie was taking it all in and it was a lot to absorb, even though deep down, she knew they were right. The ringing of Nick's cell phone was a welcome interruption from the silence. It was Katy.

"Excuse me a minute," he said as he stepped away. "Hello?"

"Were you ever going to call me again?" she demanded to know. "I graduated you know."

"Kate...I...must have started to call you a hundred times. But I could never bring myself to do it."

"Why not?"

"You seemed so mad when I saw you last."

"I know you didn't sleep with Bridget."

"You do?"

"Yes. I confronted that little slut after I saw you," she said.

"You confronted her?"

"That's not important," she hesitated, "but if you must know, I wanted to confirm that the last of the nice guys, was in fact, a nice guy. And she told me you were just dropping her off."

"I was."

"I know. Where are you by the way? Are you in the shower? I hear running water."

"I'm at Multnomah Falls."

"You're where?!"

"Oregon. It's a long story, but I'll be back in a couple of days."

"Well, you better be back before Wednesday or you're going to miss me."

"What do you mean?"

"I got the job at *Good Day LA* thanks to your recommendation."

"And you're going to take it?"

"I don't know why I wouldn't. Do you?"

"What about your family?" he stammered.

"My family is a reason *to* take it," she answered.

"What about the Assistant Producer job at *Good Morning America*?"

"They never called me back."

He hadn't expected her call and he wasn't properly prepared to talk her out of it.

"Oh," was all he could manage. "Could we go to lunch or something before you leave? Maybe Tuesday?"

"Sure," she said.

"I'll see you then."

"See you then," she confirmed.

"I've missed you," he said. But she had already hung up.

"Who was that?" Rick asked when he saw the conflicted look on his friend's face.

"Do you know anyone at *Good Morning America*?" Nick asked.

"Of course I do. Why?"

"Could you help someone get a job there?"

"What do you think? I could get Bin Laden hired as a correspondent if he were still alive."

"Can you make a call for me?"

"You want to work at GMA?"

"Not for *me*. But *for* me. As in a favor."

"So who am I getting a job for? We really need to speed this up," Rick said, motioning with his hands. "It's going to be dark in a couple of hours."

"For Kate."

"Ohhhhh," he said, smiling, the light bulb going off in his head. "Consider it done."

"Like today? She's got another job she's going to take otherwise."

"Calling right now," Rick answered as he began dialing.

"Thank you."

Nick removed a small envelope from his backpack and handed it to Melanie. "Don't open it until you're alone," he whispered as he hugged her. "It was *really* great seeing you."

"You're leaving?" she asked, puzzled.

"I've decided not to give up so easily," Nick said with a smile as he started to run back down the mile long trail they had just hiked up. He stopped at the bottom of the mountain, long enough to buy a bottle of water from a vendor, half of which he poured over his head, before he jumped in their rental car and drove away from one dream—and towards another.

XVII BETTER THAN HE THOUGHT HE WAS

"*I* can't believe that weasel left me to travel all the way back home by myself," Rick said while he sat with Melanie in the sitting area of her hotel room.

"He did leave in a hurry," she acknowledged. "Where did he run off to?"

"He ran off in search of true love I suppose. First sign of backbone I've ever seen from him."

"How long have you guys known each other?"

"About three weeks."

"Three *weeks*?! You seem like you've known each other forever."

"Some people have the ability to make you feel as though you've known them for your entire life, after a few short moments. Nick's one of those people."

"You must be one of those people as well."

"Me? Nah. It's safe to say that I'm a Grade A a-hole. What kind of a guy convinces another guy to travel clear across the country to try and break up someone's engagement?"

"Please?" she asked quietly.

"Nick thought you were the one that got away. Or I maybe I convinced him that you were."

"I thought you guys were here on business."

"Not exactly."

"But he barely spoke to me when he was here. You always did all the talking."

"That's because he's shy. And because he thought you were too good for him," he added.

"I'm not too good for anyone," Melanie lamented.

"Oh please. You're beautiful, talented, smart, funny and sweet."

"Did you just pay me a compliment?" she beamed.

"Don't get used to it. I parcel them out in small doses."

"So what do we do now?"

"Whatever you want," Rick answered. "This is your world. The rest of us are just visiting it."

She leaned forward and kissed him very softly on the lips. He seemed to be enjoying it, but suddenly pulled away from her.

"Whoa. I can't do this. Whatever *this* is."

"Wow. This is embarrassing. I guess I misunderstood you when you said *whatever I want*."

"I didn't know that's what you wanted. And I can't do that to Nick."

"Nick's not here. And he's not in love with me anyway. It sounds like he was more in love with the idea of me."

"That may be the case, but I still can't do it. It wouldn't be right. Besides, you're engaged."

"You've been trying to talk me out of that for two days now."

"I know. And a couple of weeks ago, I could have...I could have done this. But now I'm somebody's friend, and for whatever reason, he has higher standards for me than I have for myself. Maybe it's time I meet them."

"Don't look now, Mr. McDermott, but you just might be a decent person after all," she smiled.

"Let's keep that between the two of us," he said. "I'm really only a decent person-in-training."

~

It was 6:17am when Nick arrived in front of Katy's parent's house after flying all night on the red eye. Ten hours to think about what he wanted to say, and he still didn't have a clue.

"You awake?" he texted.

"I am now," was her short reply.

"Look out your window."

Nick waved an awkward wave from underneath a tree when she pulled back her curtains. She joined him outside a few moments later in a hoodie, sweatpants and slippers.

"Have to admit I'm pretty curious as to what couldn't wait until a more decent hour," she said. "I'm sure my parents would be curious to know as well."

"Oh lord. Where did you tell them you were going?"

"It's fine. They're still sleeping. I thought you weren't coming back until Tuesday?"

"I changed my mind."

"About what?"

"About everything," he answered as he kissed her—softly at first, then more passionately when he realized she was kissing him back.

"Are you kidding me?" she asked as she pulled back.

"What?"

"You waited to do that until I was 48 hours away from moving across the country? What am I supposed to do now?"

"You're supposed to stay."

"Just like that?"

"You'd prefer I waited to say something until *after* you left?"

"You might be the dumbest smart person alive. I've practically been throwing myself at you for months."

"I'm sorry," Nick said with a smile. "It just took me a while to realize you were all wrong for me."

XVIII NICE GUYS DON'T ALWAYS FINISH LAST

A few days passed and Katy turned down the job in Los Angeles to accept one in New York City at *Good Morning America.* Rick had landed her the job before Nick reached the bottom of Multnomah Falls. He cemented it by promising three guest appearances from the world's biggest female movie star.

Tom joined Nick and Katy in a booth tucked away in one corner of an otherwise empty bar. Rick entered a few moments later, shook his head at Nick with a disgusted laugh, and joined them.

"So...how was the trip, boys?" Tom asked.

"It was good," Nick answered.

"If by *good* you mean a complete and utter failure, then yes, it was good."

"Care to elaborate?" Tom chuckled.

"Let me set the scene for you. Game 7 of the World Series. Bottom of the ninth. Two out. Bases juiced. Nick is at the plate with a full count. And strikes out looking. Apparently, he was under the mistaken impression that the pitcher is supposed to hit the bat with the ball, rather than the other way around."

Tom laughed. Nick had to stifle back a laugh himself.

"Things worked out as they were supposed to," Nick said.

"Look, I'm happy for you. I kept telling you to call Kate."

"You told me a lot of things. Most of which I can't repeat in mixed company."

"I really am happy for you. Of course, if you had figured it out a little sooner, you would have saved me a couple of broken car windows, about $500 in bribe money, and a 14 hour car ride by myself."

"I'm sorry about that," Nick said. "Actually, not really. So is she going to end up marrying Bill?"

Rick checked his watch. "In about an hour and forty minutes if I'm not mistaken."

"Care to place a wager on that?" Nick responded as he slapped a one hundred dollar bill on the table.

Never one to shy away from a bet, Rick matched it with one of his own, then turned to see what Nick was staring at. Melanie was standing a few feet away from them. Nick picked up both bills and stuffed them into his pocket with a satisfied smile.

"Mel? What are you doing here? How did you find us?" Rick asked.

"Nick told me. And I guess the answer to the first question depends on you."

"On me?"

"She certainly isn't here to see me," Nick explained.

"What are you talking about?"

"C'mon. The two of you are perfect for each other. I could see that seconds after you met."

Rick was uncharacteristically flustered. "You're crazy."

"It's ok. I'm fine with it. Really, I am. Mel,

what did the note say that I gave you before I left?"

"You said we were perfect for each other," she shrugged simply. "Unfortunately, I forgot I had it and didn't read it until yesterday."

"I think Mel would be great for you. You for her?" He waved his hand back and forth and laughed, "Mesa-mesa. In all seriousness, you're probably the only bastard cocky enough to deal with dating a movie star."

"You do make an excellent point," Rick agreed.

"Of course you'd have to apply for an exemption from the Cradle Robbers Club," Melanie said.

"How old are you again?" Rick asked.

"36."

Rick winked as he pulled over a chair for her. "You got any younger sisters?"

She punched him in the arm as she sat.

"I guess I could always transfer my membership over to Nick."

"So what are we drinking?" Tom asked.

"Can I see some ID young lady?" Rick said, turning to Katy.

"You're hilarious," she responded.

"I like to think so."

Katy wrapped her arms around Nick's neck and kissed him.

"My mother doesn't like fast women, you know," Nick said.

"Then that's one thing she and I have in common. How does she feel about women who punch you in the face?"

"Don't know. It's never happened."

"There's a first time for everything," Katy

winked as she kissed him again.

Tom's wife joined them and the six unlikely friends began to dance on a makeshift dance floor. They were the fortunate ones who recognized that love was like a flickering candle on a windy night. Those that stood by and let it blow out, often found themselves sitting in cold and darkness. But those that protected it from the wind until the flame was strong enough to stand on its own, found an uncommon warmth that would stay with them forever.

They knew it wouldn't be easy. There would be bumps in the road and some difficult days ahead, but that was ok. No relationship was perfect—only love was.

POSTSCRIPT

I have long wanted to write a love story. That is a painful admission to make. But the truth of the matter is that I have always been fascinated by love. How do some people find it, when others don't? Is there more than one person for each of us, or is it as La Rochefoucauld said, "There is only one kind of love—though there may be a thousand imitations"?

How do you know when you've found that person? For me, that answer is simple. The right person is the one you can't see yourself without. But what if that person is working the cash register at a store and you end up in the wrong line? What if they are the person next to you at a stop light or sitting next to you on a park bench, but you are too timid to speak to them?

What happens to the Nick Nelsons of the world? Do they finish last? Or are there enough Rick McDermotts out there to show them the way?

Nick Nelson Was Here is a love story at its core, but not simply one between a man and a woman. It is also a story about two unlikely friends who become better people because of their friendship. And it's a comedy as they go along their path of discovery, because after all, if we couldn't laugh at ourselves, we would need to cry.

Enjoy this story? Read on for a preview chapter from another of my books, *Five Days...*

FIVE DAYS RELEASE

Imagine this. You die heroically, and you meet the Angel Gabriel. He tells you that, as a reward for your good deed, you can go back to Earth and relive any five days of your life that you choose.

How would you select five days from your entire life? Would you pick days so perfect that you wouldn't change a thing about them? Or would you choose days that required you to make pivotal decisions -- and, with the benefit of hindsight, would you now make different decisions during those days that would change the course of your life and the lives of your loved ones?

That's the dilemma that greets high school Algebra teacher Mike Postman during a particularly draining day in Matt Micros' novel, *Five Days: Which Days Would You Choose?* The protagonist, Mike, is a 40-year-old who walks along the Connecticut shoreline on an Autumn day, and he hears the faint shout of a little boy as he comes around the bend. "Mister! Mister! My friend just fell off the pier...please help!"

Mike doesn't hesitate. He throws his jacket onto the ground, kicks off his shoes, and dives off the pier headfirst. He manages to get the drowning boy over to his friend who lifts him onto the pier so that he's safe, but then he finds it's so much easier to just close his eyes, let go, and float away peacefully rather than to swim to the pier himself and save his own life, too.

So Mike dies a hero with one hitch: he may have committed suicide, and suicides are not encouraged by the management team of the afterlife. While it's not condemned outright, suicides certainly don't get treated in the same way as heroes ... except in cases, such as Mike's, when it's tough to differentiate between heroes and those who took their own lives.

As readers watch Angel Gabriel give Mike the gift of choosing five days that he could go back home and relive, we're challenged to think about which days we would select, if we could. Would we choose to have one last day with the person we loved the most so that we could say everything we'd always wanted to say? Would we elect to try to reverse a mistake that we once made? Or would we opt to simply have the experience of the most blissful day imaginable to enjoy one more time?

The character takes us on a journey through events of modern history both heroic and tragic. And on the question of ending one's life prematurely, readers are left to ponder whether suicide is always a mistake that overshadows everything good you've done for others, or whether it's just ... a choice, perhaps one that's made on the spur of the moment and wouldn't ever be a choice you could defend or would repeat. Could it be that suicide isn't enough to prevent you from entering heaven? And equally important to remember is that things are seldom as dire as they may appear...

FIVE DAYS

I
~THE END OF THE BEGINNING ~

*T*he warmth and sun-drenched days of late summer, had been replaced by the cold, darkness of November, where the crisp chill served as a precursor to a winter that would long overstay its welcome once the holidays had past. Students that were eager to learn something new and different back in August had been replaced by unmotivated, and occasionally cruel creatures that were recognizable as human beings only by their DNA.

When the bell sounded signaling the end of another particularly draining day, it was difficult to determine who was happier—the students or the teachers. Mike Postman flipped the Algebra textbook he had been teaching from closed, waved as the students poured from the room, and sat at his desk for the obligatory twenty minutes mandated by the teachers' contract.

Mike looked like he was in his early 30's, but was actually nearly 40, with the sort of generic good looks that enabled him to pass as either the clean-cut boy next door, or a Hollywood character actor. He pulled into the driveway of his modest two-story cottage across the street from one of the oldest beaches in Southwestern Connecticut. On this day, he didn't even go inside, but instead, immediately crossed to where the multi-million dollar homes stood. It wasn't much of a stretch to say that his home could have passed as a guesthouse for any one of them.

Walking on the path that ran along the Connecticut shoreline, Mike bit down his lower lip, the way he frequently did anytime he was thinking. Autumn always had a certain smell to it, he thought; even back when he was a kid. Not a strong one, mind you, but rather a soft, subtle smell, not unlike the gentle scent of a woman's perfume as she walked past. The interesting thing was that autumn smelled differently depending on where you were. In Florence, Italy, autumn was damp and musty, clinging to your senses like a memory you would never forget. In Chicago, autumn smelled like burning leaves. In New York City, it smelled like roasted chestnuts and Italian sausage. And in Woodmont - on - the - Sound, Connecticut, the smell of autumn was crisp and clean, like a freshly laundered shirt.

Gone were the rollerbladers and sunbathers of summer. Weather wise, this day was symbolic of his mood; colder than it looked, with clouds battling the blue sky for prominence. As a profession, teaching was simultaneously rewarding and frustrating. On more than one occasion, he had thought about trying something different, but he didn't know what else he was suited to do. Besides, the highs of teaching were generally higher than anything else he could imagine doing. There was nothing quite like seeing the smile of a struggling teenager after you had managed to give them some measure of hope. And yet, for every time he felt as though he was making a difference, something would happen as if to not so gently remind him that just maybe he was wrong about that.

He heard the faint shout of a little boy as he came around the bend. Barely audible at first, he was so entrenched in thought, he didn't even notice it at first. But it grew louder with each successive shout, as a boy of about ten approached him frantically.

"Mister! Mister! My friend just fell in off the pier and he can't swim! I'm not good enough to pull him out! Please help!"

Mike didn't hesitate, throwing his jacket onto the ground and kicking off his shoes as he ran to the end of the pier and dove in headfirst. It was abundantly clear that he wasn't a strong swimmer himself, but after a few awkward strokes, he managed to reach the boy.

Holding him around his neck with his right hand gripping the boy's shirt collar, he dragged him along, struggling to keep himself above water in the process. With the other boy lying prone on the pier with an outstretched arm, Mike swung around and tried throwing the boy toward the arm. Once he saw that the boy's friend had grabbed him and helped lift him onto the pier, Mike relaxed, and then suddenly, and yet almost peacefully, plunged beneath the surface of the water. For the briefest of moments, he felt himself taking in water-- through his nose, mouth, and ears. His eyes were burning from the salt water. His lungs felt as though they were about to explode. And then he felt *nothing* at all.

When he came to, he found himself lying amongst a bevy of soft, white, puffy, cumulus clouds. He staggered to his feet just in time to see a tram, not unlike one you might find at Disney World, approaching in the far off distance. It seemed to make up several miles in a few moments, before it eased to a stop directly in front of him.

"Let's go, Mike. Get on," the driver said impatiently.

"Where are you going?" he asked.

"You'll know when you get there," was the response.

How did he know him? Where was he? And why was he the youngest one on board by at least 25 years?

The tram tunneled through the clouds, emerging at the front gate of what appeared to be Caesar's Palace. Not the one from ancient Rome, but rather the one that had been modeled after it on the Las Vegas strip.

"This is your stop," the driver said, matter-of-factly, a nod of his head indicating he was supposed to get off.

When no one else moved toward the exit, Mike realized the man was talking to him, and he stepped off the tram.

"How did I end up in Vegas?" he asked no one in particular.

The response came from a voice behind him.

"You didn't," the voice said.

It was a deep, James Earl Jones-like voice.

"I didn't?"

"No. But we had to do something. We were getting too many complaints that our accommodations weren't as nice as those down below. His home looks like Graceland."

The man was African-American, wearing a white, flowing gown that was a cross between a priest's robe and a Roman toga.

"Elvis lives downstairs?" Mike asked in a perpetual state of disbelief and confusion.

"Of course not," the man laughed. "Elvis is a music teacher in Wisconsin."

Mike nodded as if this somehow made sense. "Then who's down below?" he asked.

"Beelzebub. Satan. You probably know him more readily as the devil."

"So if he's downstairs, then that must mean I'm in—"The man nodded. "Gabriel--at your service."

"How did I end up here, Gabriel?"

"You died saving that little boy's life. Or should I say—you *let* yourself die."

"I don't really recall that much about it," Mike responded, "And I don't mean that in a Bill Clintonesque sort of way."

"Your memory will come back a little at a time as you need it," Gabriel assured him.

Mike glanced around him and nodded at an elderly couple that walked past. They didn't even acknowledge him.

"If this is heaven, Gabriel, how come no one's very friendly?"

"Oh, they're not going to be friendly to you, Mike."

"Why not?" he asked, offended.

Gabriel stopped walking—took on a more serious tone now. "Because you took your own life, while most of these people has theirs taken away from them."

He decided not to waste too much time

thinking about it. He simply had too many questions that needed to be answered.

"Then why am I here, if I'm such a bad guy?"

"Did I say you were a bad guy?"

"You implied as much."

"Don't read too much into things," Gabriel answered, his tone much more cordial once again.

"And you're here because you're visiting."

"I'm visiting?"

Mike didn't much care for the sound of that.

"Is this some sort of a tryout?" he followed up with.

Mike had always hated tryouts. It didn't matter whether it was an athletic team, the school play, or a job interview. He wanted to be wanted. He didn't want to have to convince someone he was good enough.

"Of course not."

"So after I visit, then what?"

"Then you go back."

"Then I go back," Mike repeated.

"Do you always repeat everything people say to you?" Gabriel asked.

"Only when I think they're full of—"

He stopped himself just short of finishing his sentence. He thought better of it, considering his surroundings, and also how tenuous his tenure there appeared to be.

"So I get to go back where?" he continued.

"To where you came from. To any year you like actually. You've been given a great gift, Mike. You've been given the opportunity to go back and relive any five days from your life of your own choosing."

"And why exactly do I get to do that?"

"Have you ever wished you had the chance to do something over? To go back knowing then what you know now?"

"Of course. Doesn't everyone?"

"Well, you have the opportunity to do that."

"Does everyone get to go back?"

"Not everyone," Gabriel answered cryptically.

"Then why me?"

"It will all be explained to you in time. But we really need to get going."

With that, Gabriel smiled a knowing smile and held the casino door open for him to enter. Mike bit down on his lower lip as they walked past the cavalcade of high-end shops just inside the entrance, while the distant chiming of slot machines and occasional screams of joy echoed down the corridor.

"So, Gabriel," Mike said with a wink, "do they have any ten dollar craps tables at this time of day?"

"We don't use money to gamble up here."

"Then what do you use? Cars? Clothes? Women?" He winked again, and made a clicking sound with his tongue.

"People gamble for the thrill of beating the system," he answered simply.

"Don't you think it would add an additional thrill if a cool grand was riding on one toss of the dice?"

"It wouldn't matter. People have no use for money here. Everything is already provided for them. Food, clothing, shelter, entertainment, transportation..."

"Sounds like a communist block nation. Well, if they don't need money, what would be the incentive to work?"

"Most people don't. Most people have worked their entire lives and are glad not to have to any longer."

"But then how does anything get done?"

He rethought his question as soon as the words left his mouth. After all, it was heaven.

"Some people choose to work anyway."

"Why would anyone *choose* to work?" Mike asked. It was a concept he had a difficult time wrapping his arms around. Most days, he had come home so exhausted both mentally and physically, that he wasn't sure he would be able to do it again 12 hours later. Of course he always had, but if anyone had given him a choice, he would have gladly chosen to follow the Mets around the country instead.

"You yourself once said that if you won the lottery, you would still work, only without having to worry about money, you'd take a job where you really felt as though you could make a difference."

"How do you know I said that?" Mike asked. It was true. He had said it. But he was trying to impress a girl at the time and thought it sounded better than drinking beer, following the Mets and playing Xbox.

"I know everything there is to know about you, Mike. Except for one thing."

"And what's that?"

"All in good time, my friend," Gabriel said as they continued down the narrowing corridor.